SWAN KNIGHT

Fumio Takano

Translated by
Sharni Wilson

Luna Press
PUBLISHING

First published in Japanese in *SF Magazine* by Hayakawa Publishing, Tokyo, 2005
First published in English by Luna Press Publishing, Edinburgh, 2024

www.lunapresspublishing.com
ISBN-13: 978-1-915556-35-6

To Trevor Horn, CBE,
with my deepest gratitude for 40 years of inspiration

Contents

LOHENGRIN

You must not unmask me; never ask me
whence I came, my rank, or my name!

Chapter One

Back in his private royal quarters in the palace, Ludwig let out a sigh and switched on the TV. There was a cheap and nasty crackle, and the screen brightened with a buzzing drone.

He could no longer remember what the agenda for the royal council had been, whom he had granted audiences to, or which events he had shown his face at. In fact, he wasn't even sure there had been a royal council that day.

He dimmed the gaslights, threw on a change of clothes, and sank into his armchair. Ah, television. Television was the best. Wait half a minute for the big glass tube jammed inside the cabinet to warm up, and other worlds spread out before you. All sorts of dreams and all his idols dwelt within the black and white screen.

Gradually the patches of light and shade resolved into a human form, and sound came from the speaker. The box read out the news from every corner of Europe; assorted scandals, gossip, conjecture, and farce. He could travel far and wide without stirring from his armchair.

Sometimes the television even gave him useful information. It told him about the goings-on in the world, in a way that was much easier to understand and more interesting than the reports obsequiously delivered by ministers of state at that

so-called council. Why had Emperor Franz Joseph taken to
visiting a certain park of late, when he had no business there?
Who would make a better president for the Third Republic—
Marshal MacMahon or Jules Grévy? Was there any truth to
the rumour that Napoleon III was still alive and secretly ruling
France? and so forth.

There were only fifteen years remaining of the nineteenth
century. No one was free of worry about the state of the world;
it was like they expected it to end when that time was up.
And here was the television, ready to feed those fears with an
endless torrent of uneasy dreams.

At times the television lied. But he valued the dreams it
offered him far more than his reality. His kingdom of Bavaria
was a tiny, backward state, merely a mouse dangling from
the jaws of the giant that was the new German Empire. Even
when he did get accurate and relevant information, he would
find himself unable to act on it. That being the case, it was
better to have dreams, as there was no need to worry about
whether they were true or not. It was clearly so much better.
Dreams could help him forget the dismal realities of ruling an
insignificant little kingdom.

The picture was breaking up. Ludwig sprang out of his
chair to slam the cabinet with his fist. The machine heard its
king's command; the picture cleared.

Yes, television was the best. It listened and obeyed—unlike
those scheming ministers...

The fact was, being a monarch was not all it was cracked up
to be. Whenever he appeared in public, his smallest movements
came under scrutiny, and he was showered with simultaneous
praise and ridicule. He would be criticised for facing right and
so he turned to face left instead, only to be criticised for that

too. But the crowds that still gathered wherever he went were proof of his enduring popularity, and he was obliged to live up to the expectations of his subjects.

His popularity had made it impossible to go to the theatre to hear the Wagner operas he loved. While he eagerly tried to watch the stage, the rest of the audience would stare at *him*—Ludwig II, King of Bavaria, in the royal box—with even greater fascination.

Television was so much better. Ludwig could stare at it all he liked, and no one would stare back at him from the screen. No need to be dressed in a starchy tailcoat or a military uniform, no need to sit bolt upright the entire time in case anyone glanced his way. No one would scowl at him if he lounged around in his dressing gown, letting it all hang out, drinking liquor and burping.

Occasionally he would see himself on TV. He did look incredible, he had to admit. The most beautiful young king the world had ever seen. His magnificent physique, taller than all around him; his glorious waves of hair, like the hero of an epic; his stunning eyes, which were a deep lake blue (such a shame that televisions couldn't show colour!) and his smooth, almost feminine jawline.

Film clips of his coronation were shown time and time again. He appeared in full regalia, hung with medallions. In military uniform on a white horse. At the theatre, graciously acknowledging the audience; a king who was a great lover and patron of the arts. Beyond doubt he was himself a screen idol.

He was on TV so often that he lost track of when the footage had been taken. Which royal review of the troops was that again? When had he last seen the *Twilight of the Gods* at the theatre? Had he really been to France, or wherever it was?

How many years since he'd been crowned—was that last year? The year before last? It was probably about three years ago now. He couldn't remember exactly. It felt like last month, but also like decades since his coronation at the age of eighteen.

Yet the Ludwig on TV was always the perfect prince out of a fairy tale. He looked exactly like a knight of the Holy Grail from a Wagner music-drama. When he was on TV, he had a presence to rival the greatest heroes; Siegfried or Hans Sachs. When he was on TV, that is...

Ever clutching the device tethered to the box by a vinyl-sheathed wire—a 'remote control', it was called—he drifted from dream to dream. His soul plugged into the television, along with the remote control...

As he was flipping through the channels during the commercial break, a Wagner music-drama appeared on the screen.

He leapt up, knocking over the cut-glass brandy decanter at his elbow, which tumbled to the floor and shattered. Oblivious to the shards of glass at his feet, he stood transfixed, staring into the little black-and-white cathode-ray tube.

It was *Lohengrin*. What channel was this? Had it been in the programme guide? But the sketchy programme guides, carelessly churned out weeks in advance, were unreliable at best. Newsprint took so long to reach him; it crept along at a mere fraction of the speed of electricity; ten thousand, nay, a hundred million, a billion times slower. And the programmes themselves were forever being switched around as their ratings soared or slumped.

Wagner's music-dramas were the most popular shows of all. New works, fresh versions and remakes were released back-to-back: enough to saturate even the most insatiable viewers.

'I don't know this version...!' Ludwig made a wild lunge for his tape recorder, almost toppling over, and shoved in one of the audio cassette tapes he kept there, ready for use at a moment's notice. He carefully placed it in front of the TV speaker and pushed down the record and play buttons together.

Lohengrin, the Swan Knight, was battling not only his nemesis Telramund, but a host of other warriors. An unfamiliar melodic phrase, which must represent the battle, interwove with the Swan Knight leitmotif at a furious tempo. A brand-new version, with a brand-new singer! How intoxicating the music was, with its wild power and its sublime refinement! Magnificent. It was a masterpiece. There was only one person on the face of this earth who could create such music: Richard Wagner. It would be beyond the power of any other mortal!

On the glass tube, grainy black and white motes swarmed across the clashing swords of medieval knights encased in splendid armour. The badly outnumbered Swan Knight swung his sword with cool grace while chastising his foes in his bell-like tenor. This was the scene in which Lohengrin had already become a knight of the Holy Grail—though his enemies did not yet know that—and so he was now under divine protection. The henchmen of Telramund, who harboured sinister designs to take over the country, would soon find that out…

All of a sudden, Ludwig noticed that the cassette wasn't moving. It hit him like a punch to the guts. *Why?* Was it a problem with the power, the flywheel, or the motor? It should always be maintained in perfect working order. What could be wrong? Then he saw the power cord—*it was not plugged in.*

In his lurch toward the wall socket, his foot nearly landed on the shattered remains of the decanter. He twisted to avoid the glass, with an awkward half-leap, half-stagger, but his tall frame collided with the TV instead, and sent it tumbling from its gilt-embossed stand.

Save himself or the TV? No time to decide. The TV hit the parquet floor with a sickening crunch, splinters of wood exploding outward.

He landed heavily on his rear beside the fallen TV, something breaking under him with a rapid series of snaps.

The corner of the wooden television cabinet was plunged into the wooden floor. The black and white dreamscapes had turned into a grey sandstorm, and a roar of static assailed him. The TV set wasn't seriously damaged. The screen and the vacuum tube seemed to be all right. But the antenna had snapped into pieces under his body. He rolled off it, breathless with the pain, but the damage had been done.

Worst of all, Wagner's music had been silenced.

Without an antenna, the TV was useless. A roiling mass of emotion surged through him—fury and frantic impatience— and he flew into a childish rage, there on the floor. Cursing, he slammed his fist down, and under it happened to be the tape recorder, which had also toppled off the television stand. With a pathetic crunch, its cover spiderwebbed with cracks.

Ah, for God's sake. He couldn't bear it. It was all too much... Ludwig shut his eyes and put his hands over his ears. It was just too much. In moments like these he most needed Wagner to comfort him. He longed for the Swan Knight to sing.

Only Wagner could allow Ludwig to forget everything, sweeping flawed reality away in a wave of euphoria. Only Wagner could transport the audience into his stories; he dyed all singers and performers in his unique colours, with an overlapping complexity of sound and melody, and ingenious harmonies that defied imitation.

I want to meet Wagner. Since his boyhood days, Ludwig had held on to that one thought. After ascending to the throne, he had done all in his power to arrange a meeting with the great composer. Yet his dream had never become reality.

I want to meet Wagner. I want to discuss music, share our visions of legendary heroes, and grant him all the aid in my power as king of the realm. I want to meet Wagner. I want to hear every single one of his works; all the series, in all their different versions. I want to meet Wagner. I want the heroic epics I picture in my mind's eye to be staged as music-dramas at his sacred Festspielhaus. I want to meet Wagner.

I don't presume to gain the man's friendship or his esteem. I don't dare hope that far. I only want to meet him, to support him as one of his many fans, and to listen to his music. Truly, that would be enough.

I want to meet Wagner and simply express my admiration, that's all.

At some point Ludwig must have fallen asleep where he lay on the floor: when he awoke, he was chilled to the bone.

What was I doing? Can't remember. He sat up and took hold of the curtain, which was embroidered in gold thread with the slanting blue-and-white diamond crest of the Kingdom of Bavaria. Drawing it aside, he looked up; outside the window, stars glittered in the velvet black … *oh, that's right, yes of course, Wagner.* Involuntary tears spilled down his cheeks. His primal yearning ran deeper than love. Somewhere under that same sky was Richard Wagner.

I want to meet Wagner. That's all—just to meet him and tell him how much I admire him...

That's all I want, so why can't my wish come true?

Chapter Two

Ludwig stood alone in the antechamber of the audience room, staring at the television screen. He didn't know how long he'd been there.

Wagner. He must have gone to the nearest TV to find Wagner.

It was the dead of night, and the only sources of light in the empty antechamber were a dim, wavering gaslight and the black and white screen. He had been lost in the music of Wagner, all else forgotten. He had brought the tape recorder with its shattered cover, but of course it did not work. Today's version of *Lohengrin* had a lot of fight scenes; the tempo and thematic transformations pressed forward at a blistering pace. Magnificent. As the second act swelled toward its conclusion, Lohengrin, the Swan Knight, was still swinging his sword.

From the office next door, Ludwig could hear the faint sounds of another television playing a mainstream variety show. Every now and then the office clerks snuck a peek into the antechamber. Ludwig was focused on the screen, but he was hypersensitive to surreptitious glances. They were whispering to each other, but he couldn't make out any words. Probably complaining about having to stay late because the king was there.

He couldn't care less if they went home or not... But he didn't feel like dragging himself away from the TV to tell them that. In the final moments of the second act, a chord progression like that of the Flying Dutchman's storm scene was layered in, as the fight reached a crescendo. It was so cool. Television was the best. A sword fight that would look far too slow on stage could be turned into an intense battle on TV with the right camerawork and stage direction. Deep notes of tubas and trombones churned (the brass section forced to play such parts must find it excruciating!) to recreate with raw power the feel of steel armour and the clash of longswords.

Ah, how I want to meet Wagner.

He sensed someone approaching from behind, and glanced round to see who it was—a stocky, middle-aged man with a medallion round his neck was walking towards him.

Prime Minister Johann von Lutz. This man was the prime minister ... probably. Or was he the assistant secretary? A loyal man of refined taste who could also appreciate Wagner—but at the end of the day a politician obstinately focused on practicalities. He couldn't be sure, but that seemed likely. Anyway, he was certain that this was Johann von Lutz.

Lutz halted a few steps away without speaking; was he hesitant to address his king? The man seemed to presume that Ludwig would be oblivious to all around him when watching TV.

Ludwig waved him off, but Lutz pretended not to understand the gesture.

'Your Majesty, may I be of assistance?' the prime minister inquired, sounding ill at ease. 'Is there something the matter with the television set in your chambers?'

Lutz had an uncanny way of knowing whether Ludwig was acting on a whim or driven by necessity. For such a stuffed shirt, he could be surprisingly perceptive.

'It was acting up.' Ludwig didn't want to let on that he had knocked it over. They'd find out tomorrow anyway, but he didn't have to own up to it. 'The reception was no good. And tell those clerks in the office to go home. I don't need them.'

The sense of people waiting on him in the office vanished. Lutz must have given them some kind of signal.

'If you prefer, I could have this television set brought to your bedroom?' Lutz suggested.

'No, this is fine.' *Lohengrin* was already over. The version he had been watching probably had at least four acts, and each would be broadcast separately. Only the second act was on that day. Some versions could take days to watch in full. 'You may leave too. Don't mind me.'

'But Your Majesty, it is so cold here...'

Ludwig reached out for the TV's metal dial and clunked through the channels. There might still be a Wagner music-drama on.

'Your Majesty...'

'I want to meet Wagner,' Ludwig said, turning towards the prime minister.

Lutz's moustache quivered, and the furrow between his brows deepened. Maybe it was the office he held, but the man rarely let much emotion show. Perhaps he meant his vague frown to convey deep dismay.

'I said, I want to meet Wagner,' Ludwig repeated, raising his voice in his irritation. 'Find me Richard Wagner! That was the very first order I gave as your king. Has that slipped your mind?'

'Of course I have not forgotten. We are searching. But we have not been able to find him. Besides, as your loyal advisers, we must advise against granting such a man an audience.'

'How so?'

'Wagner is rather a scoundrel, by all accounts. He's a notorious philanderer, he dallies with his singers, the wives of his patrons … even choirboys, it is said; he lives in hiding from unpaid debts; he pens rabble-rousing leaflets to incite revolution. Many of his close associates have vanished under mysterious circumstances; word has it that his men wiped out an entire branch of the Italian mafia, and he apparently bankrupted a petty sovereign in eastern Europe with his wild excesses; if we count only rumours that have been substantiated, they would still number over a hundred…'

Ludwig gritted his teeth. 'I don't care about rumours. I want to meet the one and only composer on earth who can create such music; to meet him and offer him my support. He is a man of incomparable genius. Such a man cannot be confined to the norms of ordinary mortals. Conflicts and misunderstandings are inevitable. With my support, Wagner would no longer be troubled by worldly considerations and could devote all his energies to his sublime art.'

'I am not so sure about that... I wonder if he has any real need of your support, sire...'

'What on earth do you mean by that?' Ludwig felt his cheeks growing warm.

The prime minister took a deep breath and continued smoothly. 'Rumour has it that Wagner made a pact with the devil. It certainly seems that way. How can any one human being possibly produce such a vast flood of music, with radical innovations, new techniques, and fresh concepts in such

quantity? His prodigious creative output is far beyond human
power; it beggars belief.

'In the same time it takes a lightning-fast composer to
finish a single libretto, Wagner completes not only the libretto
but the full score for the opera, plus ten or twenty-odd
versions of it, and they're already being broadcast! And in the
meantime, he gives us new orchestral arrangements, stand-
alone instrumental works, arias for his heroines that didn't
make the final cut, duets for his villains, ballads for his heroes
that couldn't be tied in with the main storyline ... so much
music that it's impossible to keep up with it all. I hear that
every single day he delivers a fresh mountain of scores, essays,
and sketches for set design to his army of assistants. Sire, do
you not think it odd for a single mortal to be so prolific?

'Even if Wagner is not a scoundrel and has not made a pact
with the devil, he cannot be the sort of man it would be wise
to meet. If Your Majesty were to offer him assistance, I am sure
he would take advantage of you.'

'I don't care what sort of man he is,' Ludwig insisted. 'I
don't care if he's not the right sort, or if he's a scoundrel. I want
to meet Wagner, the artist.'

To his surprise, Lutz's usual impassive mask twitched into
an expression of cold fury. Ludwig sensed the man's violent
loathing, along with an outrage barely held in check, as if
Lutz were almost angry enough to strike him. He instinctively
wanted to step back and only just managed to hold his ground.

The prime minister glanced around the deserted
antechamber, as if to make sure they were alone, and lowered
his voice further. 'Sire, you are not in the same position as just
another loose-living noble or nouveau riche,' he hissed. 'You
must think of your station. Surely you know of the vile slander

the scandalmongers spread about Your Majesty...'

'No, I haven't heard anything,' Ludwig cut in. 'How would I know? What slander?'

This must be what the prime minister had been wanting to say to him all along. Lutz put on a po-faced expression and came straight out with it. 'That your hunt for Wagner is prompted by the same base lust with which you summon young men to your chambers…'

The shock was so great Ludwig thought it might stop his heart. A faint *thunk* sounded in the back of his throat, as if something soft had been crushed, and he struggled to breathe. What a sordid thought—how dare Lutz sling mud at the exalted existence of Wagner, holiest of the holies!

Ludwig turned away from the light of the television screen, hugging the broken tape recorder tightly to his chest. He didn't want Lutz to see the shameful flush that burned his cheeks. 'The foolish masses!' he choked out. 'What would they know of Art?' He couldn't stop his voice trembling. 'I... I just, for the sake of Art...' He needed to make it clear that his feeling for Wagner was purely artistic in nature, but couldn't find the words.

'Sire, with all due respect,' Lutz continued inexorably, 'allow me to speak frankly. Could you have forgotten, Your Majesty—the number of young men you have called to your private chambers, all "for the sake of Art"? It does not matter how strictly you command silence; the more you wish these matters to remain unknown, the more they will leak out from God knows where. Even if you pretend to have forgotten all about those beautiful youths, the masses never will.'

Ludwig shuddered. What the hell was this scurrilous philistine driving at? Had the man taken leave of his senses, or was this some kind of political machination? In truth, Ludwig's parade of lovers had not a single woman among them. But that was completely irrelevant. His yearning for Wagner had nothing to do with earthly love. He had to spell that out to Lutz; he couldn't understand why the right words still wouldn't come.

'History will vindicate Ludwig the Second of Bavaria,' he managed at last. 'Prime minister, I command you as your king. Find me Wagner!' He spun on his heel and headed straight for the door. He didn't know how Lutz responded. He didn't want to know. It didn't matter. He just had to get away as fast as possible.

In his private quarters, only the broken television was there to greet him, hissing static, a grey sandstorm lashing its screen. But a replacement could be brought in if he gave the order, and there were other tape recorders close at hand.

His towering stacks of cassette tapes all had handwritten labels in his own exquisite penmanship; every single one included the name Wagner.

Oh yes, I'll listen to Wagner. That was what would heal his wounded heart. Wagner would give him strength and restore his bruised nobility. But now he was too ashamed to even look at that sacred name. His fiery mortification forced him to avert his eyes from the broken television and the tapes. Yet the more he strove to turn his thoughts away, the more Lutz's accusations, mingled with the sensual duet from *Tristan and Isolde*, reverberated through his mind. *Heart on your heart, mouth on mouth...*

Rather than having a chilling effect, Lutz's scolding had aroused his carnal desires.

Verdammt! He must not let the name of Wagner provoke

animal appetites! But the more he forbade himself, the more unbearable the craving became. It was utmost sacrilege to invoke Wagner's music in the grip of lust. Yet this music was fire that set his desire ablaze.

Ludwig reached for the bell pull and rang for his manservant Hornig. Well used to this kind of midnight summons, Richard Hornig should soon be with him.

I will never do this again, I swear, on all that is holy, that this was the last time—he knew he would write these words in his diary tomorrow, over and over again. When had he last summoned Hornig? Years ago, or only yesterday? He couldn't recall. Ludwig felt his consciousness recede, as if crushed beneath a great weight.

When he awoke again, the sky was already bright.

His bedclothes were in disarray, but not sullied. He felt a shameful glow of gratification and wondered if someone had been with him. Hornig, perhaps, or some other man? No, he had a feeling it had been Hornig, but... The memory was gone. He held his breath, trying to gather what might have happened the night before from the sensations lingering in his body. He couldn't remember.

Bordered by its gilt frame, his painted portrait looked down upon him. *Beautiful.* He could not help but be moved by his own beauty. A thought struck him—why not have a large mirror mounted right here, in his bedroom? This was followed by a strange sensation of déjà vu, as if he might have given such an order before. Then that too was gone.

The television had been left on; a mild-mannered elderly gentleman was burbling on about tulip cultivation. It seemed to be in perfect working order. Oddly enough, he had a feeling he'd broken it last night: that must have been a dream. Like a dream, the details had faded. But it had been a bad dream, something about smashing his TV and missing out on a chance to listen to Wagner. He massaged his heavy head. Yes, it had been a horrible dream. A dream he hoped would never return.

There was a splintery gouge in the parquet floor, by the foot of the television stand. This made him a little uneasy, but a warm tide of drowsiness swept over him and soon he was asleep again.

Chapter Three

Karl was flipping through a *Lohengrin* remix, which had just been delivered to the Festspielhaus marked 'Final Version!', when he noticed something surprising—his hand froze in the act of turning the page, and he pored over the lines of music.

The huge table in front of him was covered with sheet music, so much sheet music it would make a pile taller than he was. All of it was Wagner's. Music-dramas: arranged, rearranged, remixed, or sampled. And this was only a tiny fraction of the total. No one could keep up with it all. At least, it was unlikely anyone could. Yet Karl believed that given another half a year, he would have a handle on the bulk of Wagner's work. Hopefully it wouldn't even take that long.

Karl took another long hard look at the page of the score he was holding. He was absolutely certain. This was the version that he, Karl, had arranged. But it had been approved as the final version without a single revision from Wagner himself. In fact, it was the very same score that Karl himself had penned. There could be no mistake: it was his own handwriting.

It was hard to believe. Wagner had adopted Karl's draft, the draft of a lowly underling, without making a single change!

Two months had passed since Karl started work at the

Festspielhaus as an arranger and copy clerk. During that time, he had not once met the famous composer in person. Of course, the great man would not appear before an underling like Karl, but every day a mountain of Wagner's scores were delivered.

In the vast complex of television studios grandly styled the Richard-Wagner-Festspielhaus, there were sets for every one of Wagner's operas; over two thousand workers poured in and out each day, and singers dressed as gods or heroes came and went in a frantic flurry of costume changes. The Festspielhaus was said to consume a quarter of the electricity used by the city of Munich; at least as much as all the other television stations put together, including the cable-only, pirate stations.

Electric lighting, motor-operated stage sets, hundreds of cameras to film the singers from every angle, tens of thousands of monitor screens, and powerful signal transmitters—it was astonishing that such a complex existed, deep under the ancient Bavarian capital of Munich, much deeper than the power plants and factories.

Karl hadn't seen the light of the sun for many days. So many he'd lost count. The dining hall that served as his office had bare stone walls which gave it the feel of an ancient German castle. Cables snarled over the floor to the studio and machine room next door, and a throne from a disused set had been casually abandoned in a corner, along with a papier-mâché broadsword and a goddess's cloak. The formal dining table of Italian intarsia wood—gifted by some obscure noble, rumour had it—had not been used for dining for a long time. Now it was only a surface on which to spread out floods of musical scores under the bleak electric light. The inlaid wood was gouged here and there with irritable stabs made by the metal pens of his predecessors.

Wagner was an egotistical genius, but it seemed he was open to the fresh ideas of young composers. Every day, he checked the libretti and musical ideas submitted by the conductors, singers, musicians, and miscellaneous backroom workers (like Karl); those that were judged to be of an acceptable standard would be combined into a single huge opera. Karl's job was to create individual parts for the scores assembled in this way and to make clean copies of them. He wasn't sure if there were dozens or even hundreds of others doing this same job.

But in secret, Karl prided himself on being more than just another copy clerk.

As a matter of fact, there were often places that needed work in the scores: where the music was a little thin, or the harmonic progression not quite strong enough to sustain the sublime sound. No matter how superhuman Wagner was, there must be the odd slip up as he handled so great a volume of music. At some point Karl found himself unable to let it slide—in the middle of copying out a brass part, he added several bars of his own. He could instinctively see how Wagner would approach things, even in his wildest flights of fancy. He knew he could arrange music exactly like the famous composer. In the beginning, he worked furtively, in fear and trembling, but soon it became routine. He added his own touch to every piece of sheet music he created.

Surprisingly enough, no one had ever complained. Wagner must have heard a performance or seen a score and noticed what Karl had been up to. But Karl had never been held to account for his unauthorised changes. He began to wonder if this knack for arranging music was what had prompted the Festspielhaus to take him on in the first place. Lately he'd been submitting his own original ideas to the maestro. If he could get a foot in the door, he might be able to get more creative licence.

As Karl propped the freshly-written full score of *The Master-Singers of Nuremberg* on the peeling gilt throne, the machine room door cracked open.

'Karl. Got a minute? I need a word.' Gottfried came into view. A superb conductor and pianist, he was also blessed with blond, slender good looks. He had worked on minor TV music projects with Karl, while waiting for a chance to take centre stage, before the two of them were hired by the Festspielhaus. His talent had been recognised recently; he'd been promoted from practice pianist to assistant conductor.

Gottfried held a folder of sheet music under his left arm, and the fingertips of his right hand lightly tapped its edge as if playing a piano. This was his habit when nervous.

'Sure. I'm done with today's lot.' Karl indicated the full score on the throne.

Gottfried nodded vaguely. He seemed distracted. He was always so meticulous about everything, but he had left the door hanging half open. 'So, Karl, I need a word. How are you placed ... singing-wise?'

'How ... what do you mean?'

'Do you still want to make it as a singer?' Gottfried asked.

Karl got the gist of what his friend was driving at. He had a passable tenor; nowhere near first-rate, but he might get away with it in a small country theatre. He didn't aspire to the stage, but in his line of work he'd often been called on to sing and developed adequate chops. He didn't mind performing. Actually, he quite enjoyed it. He'd taken on the occasional bit-part role and often filled in for walk-ons in operas.

'No, it's not really my thing ... not lately...' Karl hadn't been shirking his copy clerk duties to moonlight as a singer. Gottfried couldn't fault him for that. 'I was never angling to sing...'

'But you sent Wagner a demo tape of *Tannhäuser*?'

Karl started. 'Well, that was ... just on the remote off-chance, if there were a window of opportunity, that's all; anyone in music might wonder if there was a chance, I guess…?'

'Okay then...' Gottfried turned back toward the machine room and flashed a cryptic hand signal. On his cue, through the door came three of the biggest TV stars at the Festspielhaus: King Heinrich, clad in his glorious ceremonial armour; Wotan, the ancient god; and Sir Wolfram. Finally, a man with rapidly silvering hair, in a plain grey jacket—the theatre manager—made his entrance.

They all expressed delight that Karl was willing to sing. He couldn't make head nor tail of what was going on. When the manager and the superstars entered the room, he had braced himself for a tongue-lashing.

'This is wonderful. We're deeply in your debt!' the manager said, all smiles, as he shook Karl's hand. 'Well, we know you'll do us proud. You're the knight on a white horse who will save the Festspielhaus. Wagner will be most pleased. You see, we urgently had to find a replacement.'

Wotan and King Heinrich competed to shake his hand.

'Thank goodness,' said Wotan.

King Heinrich threw his arms around Karl as though deeply moved. 'So, it's decided then.'

'I'm so glad!' Sir Wolfram shot a meaningful look at Gottfried.

Karl seized Gottfried's shoulder to get his attention. 'Wait a minute, Gottfried, what's going on? Give it to me straight?'

'You're going to sing the lead in *Lohengrin*. As of now, you are the Swan Knight.'

At these words, Karl's mind couldn't yet take in what had just happened, but his body reacted immediately. He wheezed as though he'd taken a punch to the solar plexus. He lost the power of speech and couldn't even ask for the whys and wherefores.

Subtly averting his gaze from Karl, Gottfried continued as if he gathered from Karl's reaction what he wanted to ask. 'Johannes stepped down. To be honest, I don't know whether he stepped down or was let go. Anyway, all of a sudden, we were missing a leading man.'

Karl opened his mouth but as before, no words came out. *What's he on about? The Swan Knight missing—the lead suddenly stepped down or was fired? Is that a thing that happens? Sure, sometimes it does. It's nothing out of the ordinary. Sudden cast changes are a fact of life in the theatre. But...*

Karl levelled his gaze at Gottfried without blame or pleading. *It's not out of the ordinary that this happened. The extraordinary part is that my name came up at all.* 'Wait! Who did you say will be Lohengrin—me? Me, of all people? You've got to be kidding me. No one would tolerate such a mediocre Swan Knight!'

'This is no joking matter,' Gottfried told him. 'This is an emergency. Everything has already been decided, down to the recording and broadcast schedule.'

'But aren't there hundreds of talented singers at the Festspielhaus? No need for someone like me to take it on—I work behind the scenes!'

'Be that as it may,' Gottfried said, 'the theatre and all the singers have their own schedules, you know. Even if there were a singer who could make themselves available for Lohengrin for a few days, what about after that? You understand we need to fill the role on an ongoing basis, more or less?'

'But, but...' Karl's mind was racing. '...there must be a way to find someone better suited to it: how about swapping in a singer currently in a supporting role, auditioning newcomers, or poaching a promising young singer from the chorus?'

'Yes, no doubt you're right,' the manager agreed from behind Gottfried, his lips quirked in private irony. 'So, look, instead we've decided to cast a bit-part singer.'

'The show must go on, no matter what,' King Heinrich added, staring hard at Karl as if to assess the impact of his words. 'Word is that *Lohengrin* is King Ludwig's favourite. You want to give it the chop?'

Karl couldn't match his stare; he had to look down.

'That's the bottom line,' Gottfried said. 'So, memorise this by tomorrow, okay? One of the stage directors will coach you through the performance after lunch. But don't stay up all night. It's bad for your voice.'

Gottfried tried to pass Karl the folder, but he refused to take it. 'Hold on ... this is unbelievable!' Karl spluttered. 'This is completely outrageous! Are you stark raving mad?'

'In any case, you have to,' Gottfried told him. 'I know it came as a shock, but don't go on and on about it. I've been thrown into conducting and it's no joke. For God's sake, give me a break.'

Gottfried and the manager exchanged significant glances. They seemed to have formed an alliance.

Karl examined his reflection in the full-length mirror that stood in the corner of the dining hall. It was inconceivable. He wasn't bad looking enough to be genuinely ugly, but he wasn't much to look at. Narrow shoulders. Plain black hair, which he couldn't do anything with except comb it back. He was on the shorter side, if anything. On the whole, not someone destined to shine. Gottfried was a much better-looking young man.

Karl knew better than anyone that his voice wasn't remotely a heldentenor. A bona fide heldentenor voice was not just a matter of vocal brightness and range: it demanded stunning power and effortless clarity. He wasn't sure he even had the vocal stamina to sing all the way through one of Wagner's marathon operas in the first place. 'I can't do it. Not by any stretch of the imagination. I...'

'You got balls or what?' the ancient German god asked him bluntly, like a hoodlum in a bar trying to pick a fight.

Karl wasn't surprised or angered by the common insult; the only surprise was that they wouldn't let him turn down the role, no matter what he said. 'All right.' He paused. 'I'll do the best I can. But no matter how hard I try, I'll never make a proper Swan Knight. And that won't be my fault.'

'Come off it,' Wotan swaggered. 'Wagner picked you 'cause he knew you could do it.'

'Wagner picked me... I don't believe it. Did he really say that, in so many words?'

The singers shot probing glances at each other, and then looked sidelong at the manager, who kept his poker face. They nodded at Karl with evasive smiles.

'Well, that's about the size of it, isn't it?' Wotan blustered.

'Who else would make that call?' Sir Wolfram said.

'You'll get to meet him one of these days, so you should ask him then,' King Heinrich said. 'I look forward to tomorrow's recording.' He offered his hand, and as if that had been the signal, the other three also shook hands with Karl and left as they had come, via the machine room.

Gottfried went to follow, but had a change of heart and gently closed the door behind them. 'Sorry,' he said, turning back to Karl. 'Wish I could've warned you, but I couldn't get here in time. The manager mentioned that your massive promotion came about because your demo tape was circulated and Wagner wrote "This man and no other!" on it in red ink, so there's no two ways about it. Wagner's given you his seal of approval. No use trying to wriggle out of it. We can't axe *Lohengrin*.' Gottfried shrugged. 'Anyway, this is an amazing opportunity. How many tenors are there in the world who can make their debut as the Swan Knight?'

It was all down to that tape of *Tannhäuser* he'd recorded. A nameless anxiety surged up into his chest.

'Anyway.' Gottfried, who was more than a head taller than Karl, angled a long pianist's finger down towards him. 'You are now the Swan Knight. Don't try and tell me you never dreamed so big. No one would take up singing in the first place without that drive.'

To finish, Gottfried gave Karl a friendly punch to the shoulder and pressed the folder crammed with sheet music into his hand.

Whether bowing to the inevitable or motivated by secret ambition, Karl took the folder.

'So, the action scenes could be awkward as you're not that tall, but don't worry, they'll find the right camera angles.' Not waiting for a reply, Gottfried vanished into the machine room. He was well familiar with Karl's hang-ups about his looks.

Of course, Karl hadn't intended to stay a copy clerk or an errand runner forever. But this was a jump straight to the opposite extreme. It was like handing the ring of the Nibelung, the ring with the power to rule the world, to some warrior who hadn't yet earned a name even for modest deeds. But once the ring was in his hand, the world was his. Was it a prerogative—or a curse...?

Whichever it was, he had to learn the scripts for several of the versions in a single night.

Chapter Four

The first version Karl performed was very different to the original, but that was a lifesaver, as the Swan Knight had a much smaller part to play. It focused on the wild adventures of Telramund, the villain. But after a few days, this 'easy' *Lohengrin* gave way to a whirlwind of other versions; the wandering ghost of the late duke, the strange tale of how Duchess Elsa's younger brother turned out to be the puppet master pulling all the strings, and the story of how a mysterious minstrel and a prophetess stirred up chaos. Studio to studio. Subplot to subplot. He was frantic and constantly on the verge of losing his voice.

There was even one in which Lohengrin was given a love potion and fell for the wife of his nemesis (of course, it was a parody of *Tristan and Isolde*, from which it borrowed freely). But in Wagner's hands, hackneyed soap opera or pastiches were transformed into spectacular, electrifying drama.

As Karl sang, he was still listening to the overall sound. Despite his frenetic recording schedule, there were many things that struck him, both in the music and in the theatre itself. He sensed he could uncover the secret of the Festspielhaus any moment now. What if Wagner were not who everyone supposed him to be? Just as real heroes were never like those in storybooks. In stories, the heroes who did great deeds were handsome and noble, perfect in every way, but in real life, victorious military commanders tended to be ordinary men, most likely boring, pudgy old men. Come to think of it, even Wagner was—

Stop right there. He had no time to speculate. He had to learn his new part. By now he was losing his grip on what the story of *Lohengrin* was all about. But it was better not to worry about that. If he tried to remember the plot, he might forget the melodies and words he had to sing.

He'd been released from copy clerk duties, but he still managed to steal the odd moment to work on his own original music and scripts, although he had no immediate use for them.

Since he'd taken on the Swan Knight, the Festspielhaus had been flooded with complaints from unimpressed viewers. A fair few raw eggs and beer bottles had allegedly been flung at TV screens.

No wonder! Who on earth would think an underwhelming rookie like me, not even young anymore—come to think of it, I'm turning thirty this year—could pull off the Swan Knight? People were saying he'd be much better playing Alberich of the Nibelung, the dwarf. *They're right—I think so too!* But the fact that he agreed with them made it even harder to bear. *They should try it from this end... If I really could play Alberich instead, the challenge of the character part would be rewarding.*

Most bewildering of all was the news that King Ludwig was satisfied with the new Swan Knight. No one had heard this via the usual channels of gossip from palace insiders. However, it was reported on the news. The young king, gallant in full dress uniform, had appeared on TV to say a few words of praise for

Wagner and the performers of the *Lohengrin* series; the clip was only about ten seconds long.

It was unbelievable! Karl was the one who most doubted the king's words. The king had such a keen eye for aesthetics. Hardly anyone criticised Karl's singing. Even though he wasn't a heldentenor, he could sing. But he'd never *look* the part of a leading man!

He stumbled from studio to studio. From version to version. There were some patterns that repeated, he noticed, like the exact same story but with different orchestration. Some versions only had different battle scenes.

His armour was only a costume, but it made it difficult for him to move, and his movements were further restricted as the cameras had to find the right angles to make him look bigger than the other knights. Multiple cameras were pointed at him. And on thousands or tens of thousands of television tubes, the Swan Knight appeared.

It was extremely difficult to sing while fighting. Singing the melody alone would be okay, but the words...

The words...!

In that instant his mind went blank. And no matter how he racked his brain, he couldn't think of his next line. Actually, the more he thought, the more he couldn't think of it. That was always the way of it. And—

They were right in the middle of a critical scene—the pivotal battle with Telramund, the Swan Knight's mortal enemy. The orchestra, conducted by Gottfried, would not take kindly to further delay. What was he supposed to do? A few seconds passed like an eternity; suddenly one of the chorus knights standing behind him stepped closer to sing in a carrying stage whisper:

'Friedrich von Telramund, you have three seconds left to live.'

That was it! Karl sang the line, followed by the next one: 'You are already dead.'

After that it was okay. Telramund fell, he rescued Duchess Elsa, and that was the end of the first act. Mercifully, there were no retakes.

Chapter Five

The chorus knight was headed for the green room like nothing had happened when Karl stopped him to express his gratitude. Karl couldn't let him go unthanked. The knight had saved him. *More often than not, the real heroes hid in plain sight.*

The man had to be in his fifties, at least. Despite the lines on his face, he was tall and muscular, with the straight-backed bearing of a soldier. His blond hair, mixed with strands of white, was tied back at the nape of his neck in an old-fashioned manner. When Karl called out to him, he turned with fluid grace. Karl flinched slightly under his sharp gaze, but the knight didn't seem to notice; in response to Karl's thanks, he gave a friendly smile.

'No need to thank me. It's standard practice for anyone around to help out the lead. If anyone else were in your position, they would've made much bigger slip-ups any number of times. As a matter of fact, I'd heard of you long before you got the part of the Swan Knight. I think you were a sound choice.'

'Thank you,' Karl replied feebly. Praise like this was still hard to believe. 'But the viewers are up in arms.'

'They'd blast anyone who took the part now. The Swan

Knight before you was too popular. And when you get down
to it, all those people in front of their TV sets love to complain;
it's their favourite pastime.' The older man gave Karl a fatherly
pat on the shoulder. There was something remarkably calming
in the casual gesture. 'I bet those armchair critics couldn't name
a single singer more suited to the role if they tried. Imagine. If
you were Wagner, who would you pick?'

'If it were up to me, I'd axe *Lohengrin!*' Karl exploded. 'At
the moment we have a good number of gifted sopranos and
altos at the Festspielhaus; we have flexibility. But it might be
hard to scrap such a popular series at short notice, so if I were
Wagner ... I would remix it with *The Valkyrie.* That might
sound like an unlikely combination, but there's a lot I could
work with, in terms of music and narrative. And then...' Karl
pulled himself together; he'd responded in knee-jerk fashion.
'Sorry. Never mind. Forget it—you don't want to hear my
rookie nonsense.'

But the knight nodded as if well satisfied. 'No, that's
interesting. I'd like to hear more. No doubt Wagner expects
great things from you. Speaking of Wagner, have you met
him?'

Caught off guard by the change of subject, Karl admitted
that he hadn't. He immediately wished he could take it back,
but it was too late.

In this line of work, people only revealed their true degree
of acquaintance with Wagner to their most trusted friends.
Everyone wanted the others to believe that they had secretly
made his acquaintance. But of course, as there was the danger
of being exposed as a fraud by someone who genuinely knew
him, no one liked to come out and say it in so many words.
All that Karl knew for sure was that neither he nor Gottfried

had yet had an audience with Wagner, not even once. All the singers, stage directors, and arrangers made insinuations, but he didn't know who to believe.

To Karl's surprise, the chorus knight also admitted up front that he had never met Wagner. 'But look, I'm a bit-part player; you're the lead, the Swan Knight, so you should soon get your chance. It's nothing to worry about.'

'Hm, I don't know about that...'

'Honestly, it's a lot easier than you might think. Long ago, when I had business at the Munich court, I had the honour of an audience with the king himself on many occasions.' The chorus knight paused for his words to sink in, with a hint of swagger. 'Simple as that.'

Karl struggled to process this. 'His Majesty, King Ludwig the Second? You...?'

'It didn't even take that long—actually, only a couple of weeks. I had a relatively powerful position in terms of business, but that wasn't how I got to see the king. No matter how high up someone is, they'll have some kind of "back door".' He nodded benevolently and continued in comforting tones. 'I connected with the king through our shared love of music. It'll be the same with Wagner: if you can find the "back door", as a top singer, he'll be the one that seeks you out.'

'I don't want to meet him as a singer, I want to meet him as a—' The moment the words were out of Karl's mouth he regretted saying anything. 'I mean, I don't know how to explain it...'

But the chorus knight didn't show any surprise or contempt; he nodded as if that made perfect sense. 'Not as a singer? Of course. Because you're a composer,' he said with cool nonchalance.

Karl was nonplussed. He ducked his head uncertainly and mumbled some kind of reply—the older man gave him a bolstering slap on the shoulder and followed the others out.

Chapter Six

After their first meeting, the chorus knight helped Karl out several times, privately introducing himself as Hans. Backstage, he came across as a carefree dilettante.

Hans wasn't exactly forthcoming about his personal life, but Karl gathered that he had retired, passed his family business on to his sons, and then made the leap onto the opera studio stage, which had long been his secret dream and cherished hobby. Happy as a bit-part player, he could take it easy as he had no desire to advance his musical career any further than that; he enjoyed being a dilettante.

Even though the others mocked him as 'Karl's flunkey', Hans continued to support him in all kinds of ways. He explained that he wanted to keep *Lohengrin* going, since the chorus knight part was his only turn on stage, and to help Karl, the first person he'd exchanged a kind word with and his one friend at the Festspielhaus.

While Karl appreciated the support, another part of his mind was coolly calculating. Was it true that Hans had been at court? If so, he might be of some use.

People in the entertainment industry tended to be liars, as a general rule. Most people would lie as easily as they breathed, if they could make themselves look good, or more successful and important than they actually were. Karl had no connections in high places, no mentor, not even a certificate from a music school; he had started from the bottom and worked his way up to his present position in the industry, not through talent alone, but because he was as alert as a wild animal to sniff out the smallest of opportunities.

Karl weighed Hans in the balance any number of times. Was he someone valuable to know, and could he play a part in Karl's plans? His instincts urged him on—it seemed that the choice had already been made. Hadn't he begun by half-confiding in Hans? Out of Hans and Gottfried, who would be the better ally—or pawn?

However, the real world moved faster than Karl's schemes.

On his long-awaited day off, he spent half the day above ground and returned to the depths pleasantly drained by the rays of the sun. He was on a high; perhaps that was why he decided to do something foolish for once, which he would never have done under normal circumstances. He headed for an area in the subterranean labyrinth that was almost a total ruin, where no one usually went. This was where he'd happened to overhear a very interesting conversation, only two weeks ago—just before he had been given the role of the Swan Knight.

Immediately above the Festspielhaus was an ancient upper level riddled with abandoned studios and warehouses. Karl had a good working knowledge of the place, as he'd often used it as a shortcut in his role as copy clerk-slash-dogsbody-slash-errand boy. On that occasion, concealed in the shadow of a dusty mountain of unmarked tapes, scripts, and defunct equipment, he'd come across a group of men deep in a meeting, haloed by a powerful miner's lamp. That was when he overheard a few words that caught his attention.

A man with a strident honk of a voice, who seemed to be their leader, had been shouting at his subordinates to give him proper weekly reports. It had been a Wednesday. And the man had said, 'Find me a fresh face to play the new king.'

Today was also Wednesday. Karl dimmed his lantern to about the same level as before, so that it barely gave off any light, and stepped softly in the stagnant air, among the rat droppings and the dead machinery. When he pricked his ears, he thought he could make out voices in conversation, right on the edge of hearing, but it could have been his imagination. The weighty stillness became increasingly difficult to bear, and every little crunch and scuff of his feet on the gritty floor made him wince. There was the door to the studio the meeting had been held in: he held up his lantern and saw that it was half-open. Wide enough for people to slip through one at a time. He cautiously peered inside; there was a faint light and a sense of human presence there. He heard voices. He hadn't imagined it.

The instant he went to step inside, someone clasped a hand over his mouth from behind.

In his terror, he couldn't make a sound, let alone resist. By some miracle he had managed not to drop his lantern on the floor with a crash, but in spite of that, the noise of the small scuffle must have been heard by those inside—the voices abruptly fell silent, and footsteps echoed.

Karl's captor tossed a bundle of cloth, which reeked of rodent, into the studio with his free hand; he must have prepared it in advance. High, rasping shrieks erupted. There must have been a huge rat in there—more than one, at least two. The rats swarmed with feral squeals; over the curses of the man who had come to investigate, there were thuds and bangs that sounded like he was trying to kick them away in the dark.

The footsteps moved away again. By and by, the man who had laid hold of Karl slowly relaxed his grip and showed his face in the glimmer of a candle's-worth of light.

'Hans...!' Karl mouthed. Karl had never seen the chorus knight out of his stage armour before. Hans's keen, commanding gaze had a ferocity better suited to a real warrior than a walk-on TV knight.

Hans put a finger to his lips and then gave the signal to leave; Karl obeyed without question. The chorus knight led him to a passage used for transporting large props. It was wide and open, with almost no place to hide, but Karl saw why: here, they wouldn't be overheard. And if someone spotted them, they wouldn't look suspicious; they'd look like a couple of singing buddies chatting.

They sat on a wooden crate. Hans proffered a pocket flask of lethally strong spirits; the fumes were eyewatering. Karl, who didn't drink, respectfully declined.

Hans took a swig of the firewater. 'You were tempting fate, see? It's only in popular dramas or novels that amateur sleuths can eavesdrop on villains' schemes and put a stop to them, or just so happen to overhear where the treasure is buried. Why do you think we never hear of amateur sleuths coming to grief? We'd never hear, because any who were caught would all be murdered by the villains, to guarantee their permanent silence.'

For the first time Karl appreciated the gravity of what he'd been about to do and felt a chill of horror. 'But how did you happen to be there? And so well prepared...'

'I was bounty hunting. It's something I've wanted to try my hand at ever since I was a boy.' From a cloth pouch on his belt, Hans pulled out a sheaf of copper sheets engraved with 'wanted' notices and fanned them out. 'Outlaws can be turned in for the price on their heads. I get a kick out of it.'

'Can't be very safe. Another hobby of yours, is it?'

'Indeed.' Hans chuckled. 'I know how to handle myself, and I'm retired—I don't have much of a future left ahead of me. But you have a bright future. Why did you put yourself in harm's way? Who were those men? You must've had a purpose in mind. I know you wouldn't risk endangering yourself for the sake of idle curiosity.'

You're a coward at heart, that's what he means to say. He sees right through me. Karl decided to share the conclusions he'd come to, which he had been mulling over for a long while. Hans would make a good accomplice for what he had in mind. 'Maybe I should come clean... But where to start? Ah, that's right... No one knows about this yet. You must give me your word you'll keep this under wraps.'

'Of course.' Hans's teeth gleamed in the dim light. 'I love knowing a secret no one else does—don't you?'

Having committed himself, Karl launched into his story. 'That might be an even better incentive to keep it than being close-mouthed by nature. So here goes. Have you heard the rumours? That the search is on for someone to play the role of the "new king"?'

A muscle flickered in Hans's jaw. '"New king"? I've heard about that. As a matter of fact, in the green room lately, a few of the newest recruits were bragging about being shoulder-tapped to secretly audition for the role. All young, good-looking types.'

'I knew it!' Karl exclaimed. 'All the signs point to Wagner planning a completely new music-drama.'

A short silence fell between them. Karl continued, 'A few weeks before I was named Swan Knight, I sensed a shift in the theatre. There was no official notification or new script, but we all began to compete to innovate in our musical arrangements. Everyone was working frantically, as the word was that whoever stood out above the rest might have the chance to assist Wagner himself. And it was around then that I first heard mention of the "new king".' Karl paused. 'It's got to mean a new music-drama in the works. All of us would've reached that same conclusion. Naturally, I wasn't interested in auditioning for the part. My real strength is in composing and arranging. I...'

Karl struggled to put words to what he'd been feeling and thinking. He had agonised over whether to turn in fragments of musical ideas, or the draft of a full arrangement, as he'd been doing up till then. Or a fresh version of an existing script? No, none of those would be any good. There had to be something decisively different he could do. Some kind of high-risk gambit. As he stammered helplessly, his frustration mounting, Hans nodded gravely as though he had understood something.

Karl plunged on. 'The stage directors, their assistants, and even the lead singers only seemed to have heard the rumour: nothing more definite. After a few days, more and more people started to hint that they'd spoken with Wagner, but as far as I can tell, they're all bluffing.'

Speculation was rife. Everyone postured as if they were in the know. However, as no one wanted to be interrogated by the select few who *had* heard it straight from Wagner's mouth, they were noncommittal. It was impossible to tell who had personally discussed it with Wagner... That being the case, as there were still no concrete details to be had, those who felt insecure doubled down and showed off.

'In the world of the theatre, there's no such thing as objective truth. But I have proof that the speculation about the new king has a solid foundation. And that the forthcoming work will be a very special production, a departure from the music-dramas we've been working on up till now.'

There was one part that Karl hadn't revealed to anyone— not even Gottfried—yet. 'You must be wondering what the new music-drama has to do with what I overheard two weeks ago; let me explain. I found out who's behind the search for the new king: the men who are driving it are King Ludwig's aides.'

Hans let out a small 'huh', in an ambiguous tone somewhere between doubt and surprise, and his poker face gave nothing away. Did he not grasp the significance of it all?

Karl gathered his thoughts a little, and then described what he'd seen in the disused studio on that fateful Wednesday two weeks ago: the secret meeting he had stumbled upon.

He had only detected the presence of people when he rounded the corner and saw a glimmer of light from a filthy, shattered glass pane behind a grimy mountain of equipment. It struck him as fishy, but he was used to the way television types operated and didn't think it would be anything overly significant. Most likely something in the nature of a get-rich-quick scheme, a plot to dethrone someone or other, or a clandestine huddle on ratings manipulation. It would be a pain to get caught up in it, whatever it was, so he meant to pass on by, unseen.

But just as he was about to sneak away, he overheard certain words spoken on the other side of the broken glass that stopped him in his tracks. It was lucky that the lantern Karl held was one of the worst pieces of Festspielhaus equipment; it wasn't fit to light his steps. The light of the conspirators was too bright for them to detect Karl's presence.

'One of the men there was someone quite close to King Ludwig,' Karl told Hans. 'I couldn't see him, but I heard his voice. I have a good ear, even among musicians. I recognized him immediately—he's the servant of Prince Luitpold, who's in the king's inner circle. His name is ... if I'm not mistaken ... ah, something like Tillmann or Thielemann. He has such a uniquely awful voice, and the way he speaks—if you ever heard it, you wouldn't be able to forget it if you tried. Kind of like a goose choking on spoiled wine.

'About a year or so ago, we—that is, my friend Gottfried and I—were doing donkey work for a broadcaster, when that Tillmann or Thielemann came in to complain that we were using news footage unapproved by the royal household. He gave the name of a higher up, Prince Luitpold, but at first we weren't sure whether he genuinely was an official palace representative; he started shouting and carrying on like a belligerent drunk, and kicked off a huge ruckus. It was definitely him I heard.'

'That guy's not a servant, though,' Hans interjected. 'He's some sort of noble. Lord Tillmann, the lapdog.'

'You know him?'

'Sort of. Prince Luitpold is the king's uncle and the palace liaison for the broadcasters, but he has people like Lord Tillmann who do the running for him. Tillmann's the one with the twitch on the right side of his mouth, who always shouts "No excuses!", isn't he? He's so aggressive, maybe that's why he gets sent to lodge complaints.'

Hans's imitation of Tillmann's vocal tic was spot on. So, then it was true that he had been at court. Hans was the accomplice he'd been hoping to find all along!

But Karl prudently hid his elation and kept his face as casual as he could. 'Well, I don't know any of the details, like what Prince Luitpold is to the king. Anyway, the guy in that studio, whatshisname—Lord Tillmann or whoever—was shooting his mouth off in that throaty honk of his; I didn't mean to eavesdrop or anything, but I couldn't help hearing some of what he said.'

Hans nodded sympathetically and encouraged him to continue.

What Karl had overheard was basically this: 'Hurry up and figure it out, find me someone who looks like King Ludwig, I don't even care if their height and hair colour aren't the same, because it's for TV, anyway.'

He didn't know how many others had been there. He hadn't been brave enough to peer through the gap in the glass to get a good look at them. It sounded like the others present were justifying themselves in low tones he couldn't quite make out, and then Tillmann blasted them all with his usual 'no excuses' to shut them up. Karl just stood there, frozen to the spot; fortunately, the group left the studio shortly after.

'And Tillmann told them to come again next week,' Karl continued. 'You know what happened after that—I got too busy with the Swan Knight part, I was up to my eyeballs in it, but I did wonder if they'd be back the next week, on the same day, at the same time... So that's why I was there. I guess you're right: if they'd found me, it would've been touch-and-go.'

Hans, who had been listening to Karl's words as though carefully weighing each one, ran a hand over the stubble on his chin and broke into a grim smile. It wasn't a smile that suggested he didn't take Karl's story seriously, but the smile of a man who'd found a fresh source of entertainment. 'Interesting. This is getting interesting. I'm getting a kick out of this.'

'Right?' Karl said eagerly. 'So, it looks like Wagner's planning a brand-new, top-secret music-drama and not only that, it'll feature a portrayal of King Ludwig. The king's a huge fan: there's no question over whether he'd allow it. If anything, it was probably his royal command.'

Hans's smile lingered. 'I see where you're coming from, Karl. You couldn't wait to get your teeth into such a tantalising project, while it was still secret, to seize the opportunity to work with Wagner directly ... or even, let's say, become his right-hand man? In your true vocation; as a composer, not a singer.'

This all-too-pat summary made Karl want to deny it. But something deep inside him pushed aside his impulse toward self-deprecation or timidity. 'That's right. But, how can I put it... Ah, I don't even know how to describe it myself...'

'Don't worry, I know how you feel,' Hans reassured him. 'That's how it works. You're not the one driving yourself on; it's your God-given talent. You're just acting as your talent dictates. You probably don't even know what you want. It's the fate of the truly talented.'

Karl bit his lip.

'Interesting.' Hans rubbed his chin. 'Hearing your story gets me strangely fired up. I'd like to meet Wagner too. I only do opera for fun; I never had great ambitions. If I could meet the big man himself, I'd feel like I'd made it. If you're determined to chase down Wagner, let me help you.'

'That would be great but...' Karl stopped. 'I haven't the foggiest idea how we'd go about it. I don't know how we can seek him out... And now I know how risky it is to eavesdrop on palace insiders.'

'No need to seek him out.' Hans held his gaze with frighteningly cool intensity, his eyes as blue as a deep mountain lake. His gaze had such force, Karl had to look away. 'That would be a waste of time.'

'Wait a minute. What do you mean...' Karl trailed off in confusion.

'I told you I'd help, didn't I? Come on, don't leave me hanging. Imagine making yourself valuable to Wagner, more valuable than several other singers or conductors put together; no, imagine becoming his indispensable right-hand man.' Hans stood up, looking down at him, and went on before he could collect his thoughts. 'Also, have you talked to Gottfried about this? Let's bring him on board. You two are TV production pros, aren't you? We have the raw materials, we have the skills, and as long as we have the music... You'll be busy though. Plus, we'll need to secure the video equipment and supplies.'

'Music and ... video—for heaven's sake, what's your plan?'

Hans gave him a sly smile. 'We'll prepare a bait, to make Wagner come to us.'

Chapter Seven

Ludwig was roaming, as if lured on deeper and deeper into the underground world.

It was surprisingly pleasant. A world of eternal night in which blue-white electric lights burned here and there. Like the man-made grotto of Linderhof Palace. No, this underground, the authentic underground, was dozens or hundreds of times larger; immeasurably more impressive than the tiny cavern of Linderhof in which the mechanisms of the machinery could be seen. This was an ideal stage. A cavern stage. With electric lights. Vast, but closed in, connected to an infinity of other worlds. Like the inside of his eyelids when he closed his eyes.

It had taken many days of preparation for him to make his way underground. He loitered for long hours by a maintenance shed which led down underground; the lords-in-waiting, accustomed to their king's habit of nocturnal wandering, seemed to think nothing of it. When a servant's work overalls went missing, and a hunting flask and a wheel of mountain cheese disappeared from the kitchen, no one dreamed it could be the king's doing. His meagre provisions were only enough for a couple of days at best, but better than nothing.

He waited for night to fall, for his chance to escape. After a prolonged royal council—or perhaps after a tiresome evening party, he forgot exactly which it had been—an opportunity finally presented itself. All at once there were fewer guards: many of them had come down with flu. He went out into the garden, under the pretence of one of his usual walks.

Cloaked in the shadows of the shrubbery, he shouted that a stray dog had found its way in, mimicking the grand chamberlain's voice, and all the maintenance personnel rushed pell-mell out of the shed. After that, it was a simple matter to climb down into the depths from the now-deserted shed.

The narrow stair, the dark which robbed him of any sense of direction: these held no terrors. On the contrary, he felt an upsurge of joy, as if he had finally come across what he had been craving all along. It was a great feeling. He loved the darkness, and he found the slight sense of dread or the vague anxiety of being bound for an unknown destination refreshing.

He walked on, past warehouses, side doors, and enigmatic laboratories, searching for stairs that would take him further down. Fumes mingled with the gloom and the caverns began to resound with din. Unexpectedly his view opened up, and in the dim light he clearly made out an assortment of factory machinery.

The clangs and clunks of metal striking metal. Gunge and grease coated the floor. Cogs turned, and steam and smoke were sucked up into the exhaust vent in the ceiling. With no warning a factory klaxon sounded—the signal for the workers to change over. Those who were leaving their posts headed for the lifts. The sweaty, tired men were·taking the lifts down, while the fresh workers were coming up: their dwellings must all be deeper underground.

Ludwig slipped into a group of departing workers to get on a lift headed down: some of them gave him suspicious stares. The worker's overalls he wore were in pristine condition, which must seem a little odd, but there was nothing he could do about that now. The brawny arms of the men, smeared in sweat, oil and grime, and the greasy smell of their hair awoke the giddiness of forbidden lust. It was a frightening experience, swaying in the lift while closely pressed against their muscular bodies. Just as he was about to let out a sigh, the crude machine jerked to a halt and the workers poured out.

There were so many people, and so much clutter, but this was still a world of darkness, barely holding on to its sanity through the electric lights.

Tiny rooms and bars were squashed into the tangled labyrinth; a multitude of television screens glowed here and there. The men from the factory mingled with a group of women who seemed to have finished their shifts at other factories, and they scattered, going their separate ways.

The aroma of fried food. Cloying, cheap perfume. The floor was sticky with spilled beer. Laughter echoed through the tunnels. Someone was flicking through TV channels; a fistfight broke out over which channel to watch. A fast-talking host burst into loud cackles. As the workers drank, played cards, smoked, joked, or fondled their lovers, their eyes were fixed on screens. On the screens, a period drama with strange costumes. Music hall. Dreams that shone in black and white light.

Ludwig was standing there, his mind far away, when a passing man addressed him. 'You a new hire? What's up with you? Gotta problem?' He looked like a pleasant enough young man; quite a long face, but he had a friendly smile and a lithe body. As Ludwig towered above him in height, he craned himself up to peer into Ludwig's face. This was overly forward and made the king flinch back, but then he remembered that of course he too was wearing overalls, just like all the other workers, and he pushed down his discomfort.

'I, ah, I mean …'—he automatically began in High German but quickly switched to the Central Bavarian dialect the man had spoken in—'I...' He had to pay close attention to the language he used, so he wouldn't be pegged as an aristocrat. 'I'm looking for Wagner. I want to meet Wagner.'

The man briefly tipped his head to the side as if he hadn't understood, but then turned back to his companions and said to them, 'Wagner—you know Wagner? The factory boss, right?'

His friends broke into a flurry of conjecture. 'The boss is Walter, isn't he?' 'Is he this guy's friend or what?' 'Wagner, wasn't he the bookie at number 206?' 'The panel beater?' 'Johan?'

'No,' Ludwig cut in. 'Don't you know of Wagner? Richard Wagner.'

'Ah, you mean the one from TV?' one asked.

How disrespectful they were in their manner of speaking! But he mustn't blame these workmen for their lack of culture and decorum. Ludwig replied that indeed that was the Wagner of whom he spoke. He felt oddly wounded.

The men exchanged flabbergasted looks.

'I would like to go to the Festspielhaus,' Ludwig explained. 'Could you give me directions?'

Several men walked off, rolling their eyes.

'The Festspielhaus...' echoed the man who'd first spoken to him. 'The TV one? Guess it's further down, but no one really knows.' He also shrugged and left.

It stood to reason. Men like that wouldn't know.

Ludwig gave up asking for directions and searched for ways down to lower levels. At the bottom of a damp flight of stairs was a room in which drunk men were watching TV, and a desolate passageway crammed with thick pipes. Then there was a room of incomprehensible machines, set out in rows, and a room with dozens of TVs, all showing different images on their screens. The men and women there were pointing at various screens, talking a mile a minute. He had a hunch that his objective was not far away.

Momentarily he lost track of what he was doing. When he came back to his senses, he found himself sitting on a damp stone step. He couldn't remember how he had come to be there. His provisions were running low. He took a deep breath to regain his composure, clambered to his feet and began to walk again.

Unsure which way to go, he stopped. Beyond the dark glass in front of him, he noticed a shadowy human figure. A ghastly middle-aged man was looking at him. The man's bearded jowls were grotesquely swollen, and his eyes had a deranged cast to them: Ludwig couldn't tell if the man was seeing him or another world, somewhere in the far distance. Violent disgust gripped him. Ludwig hated being looked at; being looked at by such sinister eyes was even worse. It made his skin crawl. He looked away and kept walking. As he did so, the man, moving more or less in synchronisation with him, disappeared from the glass.

He felt a strong sense of déjà vu—he'd seen that man somewhere before. But where? He couldn't recall any details. Only the horrible feelings inflicted upon him when he'd last seen that man, exactly as he'd experienced just now. But the details were gone.

Pondering this, he kept moving onward at random. He went down a short flight of stairs and pushed open the door at the bottom. Once again it was a room jam-packed with TVs and equipment.

A man sat in front of the machines. Headphones on and absorbed by the screens, he hadn't noticed anyone enter the room.

Ludwig hesitated—should he pass by in silence, greet the man, or ask which way to go? He decided that to pass by was the safest option, but then he stopped dead. Several of the screens were showing clear, unmistakable footage of Ludwig himself.

Never mind the ignorant workers earlier—if this man saw him, his true identity would be revealed. He should take extra care to slip by without alerting him. But in his agitation, Ludwig knocked his leg against a table that held a tottering pile of video tapes—the recording media he longed for! The mountain of tapes collapsed with a tumbling crash; naturally the man with the headphones on turned around and noticed the intruder. He threw his headphones off and stood up in a hurry—he must be amazed to see Ludwig in the flesh. That must be it. Who wouldn't be shocked by the sudden appearance of the king himself?

When Ludwig saw the man's face, he was equally stunned. It was the Swan Knight! Definitely Lohengrin, although not in his armour. But he was a little man who only came up to Ludwig's shoulder—a bit of a lightweight. A far cry from the wonderful hero as seen on TV. Ludwig soon convinced himself that this man could not actually be Lohengrin. He looked similar, but in essence he was utterly different. He had none of the authority or the celestial radiance of the Lohengrin on TV. He wasn't even good-looking.

That's what reality is like, after all!

The fake Swan Knight in his shabby swallow-tailed coat reached back and deftly cut the switches of all the equipment. The beautiful young king vanished from the screens.

'Good evening.' Ludwig didn't know what time it was; he gave a greeting appropriate for a world of darkness. 'Sorry to have disturbed you.'

Visibly shaken, the fake Swan Knight replied, 'Ah... No, I'm sorry, I didn't realise... Wh-what do you want...?'

The man was a commoner who didn't know the proper way to address his king. No, that wasn't it. Doubtless he instinctively grasped that Ludwig preferred to remain incognito, and so he feigned polite ignorance of his royal rank. 'I don't have any particular business here,' Ludwig explained. 'I simply lost my way and stumbled into this room. Excuse me.'

'All right...' Looking mortified, the fake Swan Knight made a start on gathering up the scattered tapes. Ludwig glimpsed a label: 'King Ludwig'.

Ludwig hovered awkwardly—it wasn't as if he could help the man with his task. Should he at least ask him where the exit was? The 'exit': what exit would that be, anyway, exiting to where? To the outside world, or deeper into the underground? Well, if he was going to ask, he might as well... 'Sorry. I wasn't going to trouble you, but—I want to meet Wagner, that's all. Could you tell me how to get to the Festspielhaus?'

Ludwig was surprised at the blunt, direct words which had come out of his mouth. He had asked this in vain so many times before, and every single time he had been mocked and sent about his business.

In the end he needn't have worried: there was no time for the fake Swan Knight to answer. The other door crashed open and a man with a jet-black moustache burst in aggressively. 'Saw this random creep on the monitors. You know him?'

'Well...' The fake Swan Knight stepped hastily in front of the table, as though to conceal the mountain of tapes from the man with the moustache. 'It's no big deal, he said he lost his way...'

'You don't know if he's really lost or what. Come here, you.' Moustache didn't look that strong, but he seized Ludwig's arm with terrible force; Ludwig had a certain confidence in his personal strength and stamina, but this man's sheer power was alarming. The fake Swan Knight shouted at Moustache to go easy, but ignoring that, he dragged Ludwig out.

Ludwig tried to resist but it was no use. If he wasn't careful, he'd end up with a broken arm for his pains. They passed through a poky storage room and came out into a wider space, full of the stink of rancid sausages and beer, which wasn't really either a corridor or a room.

There were four men there whose hard eyes were like Moustache's. The men flung their cards down mid-game and surrounded Ludwig as if he were a much more amusing diversion.

'Who the hell do you think you are, buddy?' one of them demanded, with sneering contempt.

Again, Ludwig felt wounded, but he tried not to let it show on his face. 'Sorry. I only wanted to ask for directions. How do I get to the Festspielhaus from here? I want to meet Wagner.'

The men roared with laughter. All at once they began to jabber in words that Ludwig could barely follow, and to shove him about by the shoulders. 'You don't wanna fuck with us!

Don't play dumb. What station you from? Hey? Pirate stations have a code of honour! What did you come to loot—our gear? Our celebrity scoops? We'll broadcast your motherfucking snuff film!'

One of them slammed his fist into Ludwig's cheek; as if that was the signal, they all started punching and kicking. If they had come at him one at a time, he might have been able to take them on with the skills he had picked up in the military. But it was difficult all at once. He landed many blows in return, but likely due to his fatigue, his body felt terribly heavy and wouldn't obey him. Agony stabbed through his left shoulder, like he'd been hit with a cudgel. A little too late, terror engulfed him. Was he going to die here like this?

The next instant, something unbelievable—he quite literally couldn't believe it—happened.

'Stay!'

A clear voice rang out; the men looked round. A slender youth was standing there proudly, in a silk blouse and the culotte breeches of an earlier age, brandishing an archaic bastard sword. The ripples of his black hair were bound back with ribbon and his smooth cheeks glowed with a rosy flush.

For a brief moment, everyone froze. The youth was too incongruous, even absurd, in the grimy setting. The men appeared to be hesitating over whether this was somebody they wanted to fight. But the beautiful youth gazed at them fiercely and cried out in an unexpectedly silver-toned voice, 'Let him go!'

They looked all the more bewildered, but reflexively shifted into fighting stances. Showing more spirit than the men, the youth seized the initiative and charged. His sword point described an arc, and the man with the cudgel let out a screech, blood spurting from his wrist. The youth had drawn first blood. But how could such a fighter, slender as a girl, take on five thugs? Ludwig shuddered, imagining him captured, his slim wrist cruelly twisted. But one after another the thugs hollered as they tumbled to the floor, clutching bleeding arms or sides.

The youth leaped lightly across the overturned table to land beside Ludwig. 'This way! Hurry!'

Ludwig ran after the youth, down the dim corridor.

Chapter Eight

For some reason, Ludwig's body felt heavy. It was so hard to run. He was soon gasping for breath, but a rest was out of the question when he imagined pursuers coming after them. Were the men dead, or merely wounded? The youth didn't seem to be troubled by any such concerns.

They burst into a room which had a plate on the door marked SUBSTATION, and Ludwig sank to the floor, winded. He was fighting for breath. He had always meant to train his body to be functional, not just beautiful, with well-developed muscles for horse-riding and wrestling, but he had to admit that, busy with official duties, he'd shirked his exercise.

In the dim light, the youth pressed his ear to the door to listen for sounds of pursuit, and then turned to Ludwig. 'That was a close one. But why did you go anywhere near that crowd?'

'I didn't intend to go there,' Ludwig explained. 'I was lost. And what were you doing in a place like that?'

'I happened to hear those thugs shouting and realised they must be attacking someone, so I came to help. It's my duty as a knight.'

Apparently, this shoebox of a machine room was the

knight's stronghold. He pulled out a cloth from a leather bag in the corner, sat down beside Ludwig and began to thoroughly wipe his sword clean of gore and grime. As if he had no qualms about the blood of strangers.

His small, rounded nose, thick waves of dark hair, and the well-marked eyebrows that defined his feminine features... As the youth concentrated on the sword, seeming to have forgotten the man he'd rescued, Ludwig was struck by his profile. The line of his shoulders. The way he carried himself. And it was difficult to put into words, but the subtle lift of shoulder blades with each breath, the silken physique as a whole, revealed an unmistakable truth. 'Are you ... a girl?'

For a moment the youth seemed taken aback. But she didn't look up from the sword. In the weak light, she strained her eyes to make sure she didn't miss a single small nick in the edge of the blade—at least, that's what she appeared to be doing. 'Why do you think that?' she replied in a slightly scornful tone. 'Okay, I know I may look it, but still.'

'You think I can't tell?'

'Hmph. You can tell, you say? You have such a thorough knowledge of female anatomy?'

'No, that's not what I meant...' No. The opposite. He broke out in an unpleasant cold sweat all over his body. The prime minister's words came back to haunt him. *Male anatomy, 'young men'—that's what I have a thorough knowledge of.* He strove to keep his cool so as not to give himself away. 'That's just what I thought, as I myself was once a boy.'

The youth paused in her task of oiling the blade and looked at him as though her feelings had been bruised. 'And so what if I'm a girl, is there anything wrong with that?'

She must be around fourteen or fifteen years old. An age

when she would soon begin to take an interest in the opposite sex, probably. But Ludwig was moved by her open, artless gaze.

How many years had it been since a woman had looked at him without a hint of flirtation? It might even be a first. It may have been well-nigh impossible to turn a pure gaze on Ludwig, born to shoulder kingly rank. There was no escape: when he concealed his rank, he was subjected to oglings of commonplace, garden-variety lust because of his stunning good looks. Females were troublesome creatures, he thought. As women went, even the one he ought to hold in the highest esteem, the Austrian Empress Elisabeth—because their family tree was so convoluted, he was not sure whether she was his first or second cousin—even with her, he caught glimpses of innate female vulgarity.

But the young swordswoman's look was so straightforward he flinched.

'No, of course there's nothing wrong with that,' he replied. 'It's just that I have never before seen anyone, man or woman, as skilled with a blade. I simply marvel at the fact that you are female. If I have caused offence, I beg your forgiveness.'

The young swordswoman thanked him frankly and returned to caring for her sword. Judging by her slight accent, she must be from foreign parts. Perhaps from the New World. Somewhere far away that he was not acquainted with—a fairy tale land. Her unconventional behaviour, which in Bavaria was wildly improbable, might be not unusual there.

She sheathed her blade, somewhat reluctantly, and turned back toward Ludwig. 'Do you know what kind of place that was?'

'No, I have no idea,' he admitted.

'One of those so-called pirate stations, that pump out

uncensored extreme content by cable. A place like that would give anyone the willies. I'm an extra-slash-errand runner at a slightly better station. I just happened to be passing by. Anyway, you said you were lost; where were you trying to get to? If I know it, I'll take you there.'

'I'm searching for the Festspielhaus. I want to meet Wagner.' He'd been rebuffed every single time he'd asked for directions, but drawn in by her frankness, he ventured to ask one more time. It might have been more prudent to hold out a bit longer and see how things went...

But to his surprise, her face lit up. She put her sword down and leaned forward a little, looking at him again. 'What a coincidence—I'm looking for the Festspielhaus too! But those in the know don't like to give away their hard-won secrets to newcomers. Maybe we can help each other!'

She seemed far too open and trusting.

'Sorry, I haven't even told you my name yet,' she went on. 'I am Parsifal, a knight of the Holy Grail. Of the fellowship of Tristan and Lancelot.' She held out her hand, which was slender but had extraordinarily strong bone structure.

If one were to stand on ceremony, her manner was presumptuous, but he took her hand. 'I am Ludwig. King of Bavaria...' He shut his mouth, inwardly cursing his own stupidity, but it was too late. For God's sake! His 'disguise' was flimsy enough as it was; apart from the worker's overalls he wore, it was glaringly obvious that he was the king.

But the girl who went by the name of a knight of the Round Table clasped his hand with a delighted smile. Or was it a bold grin? 'Oh right! Yeah, I get it. Your Majesty, I heard you were a fan, so I'm not surprised you want to meet Wagner! I want to meet him too. I bet I could be of service to him. I don't think there are many singers out there who can genuinely use a sword...'

Ah, so that's what she has in mind. She must be planning to use that angle to sell herself as a singer to the Festspielhaus.

'Call me Parsifal. How shall I address you, milord?'

'Ludwig is fine. It's a common name. And of course, I don't want anyone to find out who I really am.'

'Good point. Ludwig, I've got your back! Let's go find Wagner!'

Ludwig nodded. He couldn't say why, but with Parsifal at his side, he felt he might have a real chance to succeed in his quest.

Chapter Nine

Karl had found a successful strategy to cut down the time he spent performing as the Swan Knight.

As a librettist and composer, what he came up with was to submit an endless succession of scores for flamboyant soap operas centred on Elsa von Brabant. All of them were over-the-top, syrupy melodramas aimed at the petit bourgeois wives who loved daytime television. When a despicable scheme forced Elsa to give up her ducal rank, she became lady's maid to a princess. By an odd twist of fate, Elsa and the princess had the same father. The bullying and violent words showered on Elsa by her half-sister, their love and hate for the Swan Knight ... those were the aspects that bumped up the ratings.

Every last one of Karl's ideas were based on stories he'd heard somewhere or other, but he didn't care.

He also created a version in which Duchess Elsa was much older than Lohengrin. In this version, Elsa was mistress to the German king, but she fell hopelessly in love with Lohengrin, the son of her first crush ... this wasn't an original plot either. Despite the hackneyed subject matter, in the hands of Wagner this too was transformed into a mighty epic, as usual.

Wagner adopted the vast majority of the ideas Karl came

up with—in fact, almost every single one. It wasn't a stretch to say that the great man seemed to be dancing to Karl's tune. Of course, Karl deliberately varied his penmanship and the stationery he used; he didn't sign his work, and he even asked Gottfried to copy out scores for him a few times. He took great care to hide that the scores were all the work of one person—himself. He didn't know whether Wagner had really been deceived by these tactics, but incredibly, none of the stage directors, conductors, or Karl's rivals caught on.

No one noticed what he was up to. With just one exception.

Whenever their paths crossed backstage, the theatre manager reminded Karl to focus on his role as lead singer, as he was excused from all other duties. As far as his co-stars and certainly the stage directors were concerned, Karl had nothing to do with the sheet music. So why did the theatre manager feel the need to remind him that he didn't have to work on scores anymore? Had he figured out that Karl was still busily arranging and remixing? As a result, Karl took even greater care to disguise his handwriting.

Arranging and song writing weren't easy, but they suited him a lot better than the inexorable grind of performing as the Swan Knight. At least he could work independently and didn't have to deal with other people when he worked on scores.

His new strategy had an unforeseen knock-on effect: following his lead, all the other composers fought to create spin-off versions of *Lohengrin* that featured characters other than the Swan Knight. This was very effective. In the breathing space thus created, Karl set to work on the 'bait' that Hans had proposed.

Gottfried came to an understanding with a TV station—one of the bottom-feeders that offered pay-by-the-hour studio time and cable distribution. Their equipment was a joke, but it was important to use a station that wasn't shady enough to risk a run-in with the authorities. Hans liberally provided funds.

The bait that Hans wanted Karl and Gottfried to create was a total surprise. Actually, it was the material he provided them with that was the real shock. This was a number of video tapes. The labels on their spines stated bluntly: 'King Ludwig, material'.

The king riding. The king in the seat of honour at the theatre. Scenes of him attending international conferences and banquets; walking the streets in civilian dress, that is to say, incognito; dancing awkwardly at a ball: the kind of footage that the palace would never make available for public consumption. At least, it was highly unlikely to be fake footage made with a body double. It wouldn't be logistically possible to film in such a variety of sets and costumes, with cameos by so many foreign sovereigns.

What most intrigued Karl and Gottfried was that it all looked as though it had been filmed on hidden camera. The resolution was low; it had obviously been captured with a small camera, not a TV camera. All of it was from odd angles. And the audio tracks had been deliberately erased.

Before Karl could get a word out, Hans shut down any questions by telling him, 'Just grab the bits that look good and edit them. There's a bit where he sings with a music tutor somewhere in there—use that. For the music, anything by Wagner would work, or a pop arrangement of Wagner.'

That was what they were up to: editing the unauthorised royal footage to create a promo video for a new singer identical to King Ludwig.

Karl and Gottfried looked at each other.

'So, who's going to perform it?' Karl asked.

'You can sing and Gottfried can accompany you. Add effects, get creative with how you sing, dial down the image and sound quality to look like a pirate video, and I doubt anyone will figure out it's you. They'll be too distracted by the royal montage.' Hans told them he had smuggled a piece of British equipment into the pirate station. This was a device that could alter the frequency or quality of any sound as desired.

Hans talked a good talk about how interesting it would be, how they'd all get a kick out of it, but Karl inwardly cringed at the risk.

'Be that as it may...' Gottfried sounded even more sceptical than Karl. '...say we put this music video out there, how do you expect them—the palace, or Wagner, or both—to react? If they do happen to see it, then what?'

'They'd make inquiries at the pirate station,' Hans replied smoothly, as if this were a foregone conclusion. 'After that, I want you to leave it to me. I have it all worked out. If we stand to gain anything from this music video, it should go to you two. I only want to meet the famous Wagner, that's all. I'm in it for the hell of it.'

Hans handed over the precious tapes to the two of them, with an air of generosity and a grin that showed he was having the time of his life.

Karl hadn't been freed from the role of the Swan Knight, although it had gotten easier. But their new project began to consume him to a degree that he found surprising. He extracted clips from the footage which couldn't be identified as the real king, edited them, and sometimes used the tall figure of Gottfried to film connecting scenes. When filmed from behind, or with backlighting, it was surprisingly difficult to tell them apart.

Karl remixed Wagner into a pop arrangement. At first, he had a single keyboard part in mind, played by Gottfried, but then he realised that he could produce a track as if a small orchestra were playing if all three of them did multiple recordings on different instruments. By multi-tracking, Karl alone could create a whole chorus.

Karl sang lead vocals, of course, but he was quite confident no one would ever know it was him. Thanks to the British device Hans had sourced, he could completely transform his voice quality. Britain! Clearly she was a special country whose industrial revolution had rocketed ahead. The device worked like magic. He could do whatever he liked with the sound waves. It was unparalleled. Rule, Britannia! Britannia rules the waves!

This was no time to wax lyrical; he had to concentrate.

Completely absorbed in his work, Karl did not notice the presence of an intruder. Focused on the King Ludwig video he was in the middle of editing, he was slow to realise that a strange man in ill-fitting worker's overalls had entered the studio. The grossly bloated, jowly intruder was whisked off by the pirate bouncer, but a scuffle ensued and apparently he escaped the pirates' clutches.

If only the man didn't blow their cover, they should be able to keep everything under wraps. And Karl thought it was safe enough. The man hadn't taken any interest in the hidden-cam footage of the king; he had only said, with a faraway look, that he wanted to meet Wagner.

Karl found it hard to get the incident out of his mind; he

wondered about the strange man from time to time, as he mixed and edited.

With cable television, the further away the base station was, the more the picture and sound quality dropped. This couldn't be fixed unless an ultra-low resistance cable—or some other ground-breaking innovation—were to be developed some day. But this now worked to Karl and his friends' advantage. No matter how the device processed his voice quality, he wasn't expert enough to significantly change the way he sang. Some viewers commented on the similarity, but no one had found out that Karl was actually the one singing.

The non-existent new singer ('Ludwig') only had his video clips broadcast sporadically on the pirate station, but it seemed he had already drawn the attention of a few discerning viewers. It was less than a week since he had first appeared, but here and there Ludwig's name was cropping up at the Festspielhaus. It wasn't a dramatic burst of popularity, but it would do, as their real targets were Prince Luitpold and the great Wagner himself.

If things went sideways, there was also the possibility that the real King Ludwig would take the bait...

Hans just grinned and said that was fine by him. At some stage he had become their unquestioned leader.

'Wish there was a shorter version of the Tannhäuser overture,' Gottfried muttered, as they watched a clip of King Ludwig hunting. 'We could do it as an arrangement... But ideally I'd like that full orchestral sound.'

'If we can record all the parts of the orchestra on separate tracks, we can edit them together and do whatever we like,' Karl replied listlessly. Yes, in theory it was possible. It was just that they hadn't yet been able to push multitrack that far. Ah, if only there was a device that would let them easily add, alter, and tinker with all the sounds…

People were shown illusory things on TV; they dreamed of what they could never have. They craved things that they couldn't be sure existed.

Karl called to mind the intruder's eyes. The strange man who'd said he wanted to meet Wagner. Karl hadn't told Gottfried or Hans about that minor incident. *Those eyes...* The eyes of a man who had visions, dreams; a tragic figure fuelled by unrequited longing. Karl had sensed that. Eyes that didn't see what was really there in front of them; eyes that gazed into another world. Eyes that bordered on madness, and those bloated features. *Those eyes...* The man had been ugly, but if someone had explained that this was the beautiful king after decades had passed, he might almost believe it.

'Hold on...' Karl began.

'What is it?' Gottfried asked.

Karl didn't reply. He couldn't. It was such a stupid question, it would be embarrassing to ask. Well, maybe it wasn't so stupid after all.

'What is it, Karl?' Gottfried repeated.

'Nothing, never mind. It's just... I wondered whether it might be time to head back to the theatre.'

Hans glanced at his pocket watch and agreed. As they walked, Hans and Gottfried chatted about goings-on in the theatre, but Karl didn't say a single word. The whole way, he was trying to figure something out.

How many years—or decades—had it been since King Ludwig ascended to the throne?

Chapter Ten

Once the Cabinet meeting was over, Ludwig returned to his room to watch TV. He dimmed the lights, sighed with relief; when he switched the TV on, it lit up with a cheap and nasty crackle.

Come to think of it, had there really been a Cabinet meeting that day? He had a feeling he might have been wandering in the underground world all day. But as the cathode ray tube warmed up, frizzling gently, the thought itself—'Which was it: meeting or underground world?'—was already gone. And soon after that, he no longer wondered why the underground was so comfortably familiar to him.

The screen brightened with a low, buzzing drone. There lay his black and white dreams; every conceivable idol, ready to be worshipped.

Ludwig stared into the small television set on its cheap stand. Ever clutching the device tethered to the box by a vinyl-sheathed wire—a 'remote control', it was called—he drifted from dream to dream. His soul plugged into the television, along with the remote control...

The picture quality wasn't great, but he was fascinated by all the channels he hadn't seen before. Pirated Wagner, reruns, theatre camrips, fan-made videos and remakes—things he'd never imagined. Ridicule of the nobility that was not usually voiced openly, dirt on foreign governments, risqué gossip, explicit sex, and...

He was watching a beautiful youth in the cathode ray tube when he realised Parsifal was standing right behind him. Sweat broke out all over his body and he hastily changed the channel. He lied, explaining that he had dozed off, exhausted by the long, drawn-out Cabinet meeting, but she looked sceptical. To his surprise, she asked if he remembered any of the people they had met on their travels that day.

It was his turn to get suspicious. What the devil was she talking about? Swamped with official duties, there was no way he'd have the time to be gallivanting around with her. In the daytime—although he only knew what day and what time it was from the TV—he had no idea where she went or what she got up to.

His first impulse was to refute her absurd claim, but he thought better of it. It was folly to expect a commoner to understand the duties of the crown. And the way she insisted they had spent so many hours together—it must all be a fantasy born of her adolescent neediness. Better leave her be. Might be wiser to go along with it, if possible.

However, a small corner of his mind recognised that she spoke the truth: they had been journeying through the underground. There were even times when he worried that he might not really be a king. Maybe he was a little too much at home in the underground world.

He had rented these lodgings (cramped, but there were two rooms) with the silver coin he'd brought with him; of course, he hadn't brought any gold, as that would give away his noble identity. The crude, battered tables and round stools of a sort found in dive bars, the small TV balanced on a warped board, the foetid straw pallets, the rust-coloured couch that had faded without exposure to sunlight—all of this was intolerable, and the festering mood of the place strangely galvanised him. It was beyond redemption … humiliating, oppressive, hopeless. Like an itch he had scratched till it bled, resentment welled up from the irritation of his surroundings.

He clung to thoughts of Wagner. He had faith that if only he could endure these squalid surroundings, as his just reward, surely he would deserve to meet Wagner at last. The worse the circumstance, the greater the reward for enduring it. He would be willing to suffer much worse to prove his devotion.

I want to meet Wagner.

A conventional Italian-style opera was on TV. Parsifal was drawing a map on a worn, crumpled piece of paper, taking care not to pierce right through it—a map of the underground world, albeit a very local one. A den of engineers. The lodgings of strumpets. A nest of rundown studios. Stashes of bootleg moonshine. Pipework.

Most of the paper was blank, but Parsifal wasn't fazed by that. It didn't matter because her one goal—*their* only goal— was to reach the Festspielhaus.

Ah, how I want to meet Wagner!

The drainage tunnel they were walking along, lit up by Parsifal's lantern, was rank with the competing stenches of sewage and oil.

'It's a funny thing, isn't it, to fall in love?' she said, as though to herself.

The two of them had wended their way through the

passageways of a black-market cable seller to sneak into this tunnel, although Ludwig had forgotten how long they'd been down here.

'If you love something so much you can't bear it, what are you supposed to do? If you fell in love with a picture, could you be satisfied if you were looking at it—would that be enough? What if you owned it? But I wonder if that could really satisfy the urge. How about a novel you love—do you think it's enough just to read it? The person you love—if you slept with them, would that be all you need? Would you be truly satisfied if you married them? But here's the strange thing: you might get tired of them. If you didn't ever get tired of them, maybe you could be satisfied then. But to go on loving forever without ever getting tired would be so hard... What if the weariness settles in when it gets too hard to keep loving so intensely, as a relief from the pain of that love?'

Ludwig kicked a dead rat down into the drainway and scanned the walls ahead for any branches leading off the main tunnel. 'But I don't like the idea of getting tired,' he said. 'It would be unbearable. To lose the love you'd had until then; that would leave behind a terrifying emptiness.'

'True...' Parsifal had turned away, her face in profile twisted as if she were in terrible pain. 'I think so too. Love is hard to bear, but I don't want to be set free from it. You're right... Music, what about music—is listening to it enough? Would performing it satisfy the craving? What do you think? I long to perform the music I love, the same way someone else might long to kiss their beloved, but when I sing, sometimes it's too much for me. I feel the music so close to me, but it still isn't mine. And the other thing with music is that it slips further out of reach as time goes on...

Anyway, why do you think we are driven to love like this—'

Parsifal's words circled back around to the same places over and over, like the maze of interconnected tunnels; in Ludwig's mind too, his thoughts moved in circles.

Yes, that's right. I want to meet Wagner. I'm here because I want to meet Wagner. But what will I do if I meet him—commission him to turn my favourite story into a music-drama? Can royal prerogative control a lawless artist? Nay, would he listen to the plea of an ardent admirer? If we succeed, will I be satisfied?

Somewhere far away, deep in his hazy, weary consciousness, a swan knight sang on a black and white screen. Lately the Swan Knight wasn't on as much. Elsa's over-the-top melodramas rolled on, day after day. But that was classic Wagner. A syrupy melodrama, with an outrageous script as its main selling point, could be transformed into a tragicomedy of profound depth and heroic destiny merely by adding his music.

Parsifal's map expanded, bit by bit.

The only thing that really bothered Ludwig was that he couldn't record Wagner's music-dramas. *Should I have brought a tape recorder? No, I know what would be much better...*

Ludwig recalled the studio where he had seen that fake Swan Knight. *...that's right, the video recorder there at the TV station: the video deck!* That would be so much better than recording on cassette tapes. He would just need to have the Cabinet sign off on its installation in his royal bedroom. It would be easier to get approved than a new extension to the castle. Why hadn't he thought of it before?

Actually, a while back, a chamberlain, or the royal household staff, or the Cabinet had once ... no, that wasn't right—hadn't he given this exact same order many times?

He couldn't remember.

On the screen, in an invincible physical form created with cutting-edge technology, Princess Isolde was fighting her way out of a castle filled with monsters. Duchess Elsa's younger brother wasn't dead; he went off by train to a school of magic. Warrior-chief Hunding, armed with mechanical appendages like octopus tentacles, faced off against Siegmund, who had gained special powers after a spider bite. Eva went to rescue Walther the singer, who had been spirited away to an underground labyrinth.

'Hunding is dead. Why?' said Wotan.

In answer, Siegfried muttered, 'Because he was a mere boy.'

Revived by cat magic, Brünnhilde—

Anything was possible on a black and white screen—dreams, idols, all at his disposal. Ludwig's eyes were locked on it. Pleasurable fantasies throbbed from the warm glass tube. He stared at the screen, in the same way young girls would watch a fake war documentary before heading off to ply their sleazy trade. As disabled soldiers watched a kids show. As an elderly couple were bombarded with ads for high-fashion accessories. As mama-sans peered at a still shot of a twisted corpse in advanced decay. As a lonely lighthouse keeper saw the smile of a foreign emperor. As a misanthropic child watched a formal ball held years ago. As a coachman with haemorrhoids saw a new work by Wagner. As an aristocrat, who secretly had to work to make ends meet, lusted over a girl's thighs in tight close-up. As ageing rent boys watched a pirated show on the genius of Bismarck.

At some point, Ludwig found himself standing in the corner of a factory with Parsifal. She was asking the workers for directions. Machinery growled low; when he looked across at the glass that formed a boundary between this room and the next, a big, bearded man with puffily-swollen features was staring at him from behind the glass wall, an odd, wild look in his eyes.

It was like he was seeing the man for the umpteenth time, but who could he be? He even felt he knew him quite well, too, but couldn't remember how. Whenever he saw the man, he hovered on the verge of remembering something or other, but it always eluded him. Something ... something he didn't want to remember.

At the back of a musty studio, Parsifal was wiping blood from her sword. 'Composers are not necessarily the best interpreters or performers of their own works, are they?' she mused. 'Someone else's performance could be much better than the composer's. I wonder why that is. Here's what I think: it's the passion the performer has for the music... I mean, it's because they're so in love with it. And even if they perform that music, it will never belong to them. Even if the composer promised to gift that song to them ... it wouldn't work. The song can never truly be theirs...'

She wore a new silk blouse, but her right shoulder was gashed and oozing blood. What had happened? When had she been injured? He couldn't recall. But he winced to see the wound on her girlishly pale skin, exposed by the rent in the silk.

Ludwig removed his cravat from around his collar and wrapped it around her shoulder to staunch the wound. He wasn't wearing the worker's overalls: at some point he must have come by these clothes, which had a more gentlemanly air about them. Parsifal thanked him, in such a tiny voice he could hardly hear her; she was not pleased. If anything, she seemed afraid of being hurt.

Ludwig swiftly understood her hesitation. It was risky to accept the kindness of a relative stranger. That's right, because then you ran the risk of losing that kindness. She was truly a kindred spirit.

'I'll protect you,' she said without looking up; she continued to write on the map, nursing her shoulder with the dressing on it. 'Because you're my friend.'

On the TV, Lohengrin was on his way to rescue Elsa from an underground labyrinth.

Ludwig was in good spirits. The haze of confusion was most enjoyable to lose himself in. However, he couldn't stand the fits of sentimentality that seized him every now and then. *I want to meet Wagner.* At that very instant, another man must be meeting with Wagner, taking instructions from him, singing for him, being lauded for the opera's brilliant success, accepting a cup at his banquet, and Wagner knew that man's name. It was unbearable. Some other man had weaselled his way into Wagner's good graces; some other man was loved by Wagner. The thought alone drove him wild with jealousy and impatience. His unrequited heart bled.

I want to meet Wagner.

But if I open the royal coffers to him and build a theatre for him, would that satisfy me? In the first place, would Wagner, who raked in huge sums for TV sponsorship, allow himself to be bought by a particular monarch?

If only Ludwig were not a king but a musician instead. He would sing one of Mastersinger Walther's arias, and Wagner would be profoundly moved. Merely imagining the scene made him swoon. It would be ecstasy. But this was a dream that could never come to pass.

He couldn't bear it. As he sat here, thinking these thoughts, he was aging, and so was Wagner. When they finally met, the two of them would be old men already put out to pasture, careworn and haggard, and to shake hands stiffly might be all they could manage. He didn't want that. *I want to meet Wagner.* He had to meet him right away. He would move heaven and earth to meet the composer in his prime with still so much to accomplish, and while he himself was still a young king. Inspired by Ludwig's ideas, Wagner would bring forth a completely new music-drama. They would talk about Art all night long, co-create, and Wagner would tell him, *I can no longer conceive of a new work without your inspiration.* And the two of them would meet on the level of Art, united with a special bond beyond the understanding of the vulgar prime minister and the unromantic world.

Ludwig didn't know how he knew, but he was sure he was getting closer. So, then, why did he feel sadness creeping over him? As if he were on the verge of something he didn't want to remember?

'What's the matter?' Parsifal occasionally asked him, in the tone of a physician. In the tone of an alienist... Like the alienists who had come to see his brother, Otto, when he had lost his grip on reality.

Ludwig would reassure her that he was fine. 'Nothing. Mayhap I am wearied by the royal council. Today ... what was it today? I think it's simply the fatigue of attending to all those old-fashioned ministers. I can't put my finger on it.'

Parsifal looked sombre. Why was she gazing at him with so much concern? With compassion and sympathy in her eyes. 'You know, today we were still trying to find a way under the power plant ... but never mind. Don't worry about it. It must be difficult because no one understands... But I've got your back. We're buddies,' she told him with unabashed sincerity.

Had he ever heard words so sincere from a creature of the

female persuasion? Deep inside his mind, in an obscure corner that usually he never even glanced into, there was a glimmer of light.

Switching from channel to channel. His eyes were dry and burning.

He mustn't dare to dream. All at once, something was holding him back. That's right, there was a jinx on him that meant that not one of the dreams he cherished would come true. He mustn't forget the jinx. The more he wanted these dreams, and the more important they were to him, the more he had to put them out of his mind.

'You think? But what if the jinx was meant to be broken? If the first wish that ever came true was the most important one? Like a princess sleeping in the woods, waiting for her prince,' Parsifal said, as she gave the hissing, dark-snowy-screened TV a bash with her fist. 'If your dreams could never come true, I actually think that would be much easier. A dream that might come true, or might not come true... I think that's the hardest to bear.'

The television obeyed her; the screen brightened.

Someone was singing—it was Erik's Cavatina from *The Flying Dutchman*. It was a shamelessly pop arrangement, remixed with the latest dance beats, but Ludwig was captivated by it. The singer sounded just like the new Swan Knight who had taken on the part recently. But what really shook him was the music video.

The singer bore a striking resemblance to himself. No, the singer *was* him. Actually, it might really be him. A vague memory of singing just like this floated into his mind.

In a blue and gold salon, the on-screen Ludwig was pensively turning the pages of a small book, his legs propped on a crimson velvet footstool; his hair was neatly combed to either side, accentuated by soft curls below the parting on the right and above his left temple.

The picture was black and white, but he could recollect the colours. The on-screen Ludwig's fingers were remarkably sinewy compared to his fine features; they curved lightly on the book, like a pianist poised to play a technically demanding piece. When he spoke a word or two to someone off-screen, the camera zoomed in on his exquisitely-sculpted cheekbone, which modelled the perfect soft ridge that ancient Greek sculptors had desperately striven for.

The word 'beautiful' had been formed for that moment.

The singer, Ludwig's doppelgänger, stood beside a piano with his backlit face obscured by an enigmatic halo of light.

Ludwig was about to remember. A memory like the stare of a hideous middle-aged man from behind dark glass.

'Guess what?' Parsifal said, brimming over with excitement. They were negotiating a tunnel that was crammed with discarded equipment. 'There's some buzz in the TV community that Wagner is looking for someone to cast in a new king part.'

Ludwig felt his irritation rise out of all proportion. *Wagner*. This little Pollyanna had no idea how painful it was for him to hear that name. 'Why the sudden change of subject? How little you know of good manners.'

'Sorry ... but ... oh, no, never mind. My bad. Yes. Sorry.' Parsifal apologised with such good grace, it was touching. Under the lantern's light her cheeks were faintly flushed.

Why was she looking at him like that? With pity—no, with compassion. With eyes like those of Our Lady of the Deposition of Christ.

Where was he? He couldn't remember.

Chapter Eleven

Karl lounged on the papier-mâché throne, leafing through scores that were covered in the scrawls of many different hands: bits and pieces scribbled by his colleagues, ideas confidently tagged with signatures writ large, drafts which were a plagiarised mishmash, and corrections made in bold red ink. He cast his eyes swiftly through the bundle of music, biting on his pen in lieu of a pipe.

There was no more room for doubt. It was just as he had thought: the Festspielhaus was sitting on a sensational secret. It was incredible that no one else had noticed.

Far beyond the circle of electric light where he sat, a distant door creaked open, followed by the echoes of familiar boot heels on stone. He slipped a few pages to the back of the pile, stood up with a theatrical sigh, and continued to sort through the scores.

The theatre manager approached the intarsia table and gave a self-conscious cough for attention, as Karl was pretending not to notice him.

Karl kept on sorting the sheet music into a pile of final drafts to be sent off to the copy clerks, and finally reacted to the manager's second cough. When he looked round, the manager gave him the smile of a mid-ranking bureaucrat caught in a dilemma. 'Oh, sorry,' Karl said. 'I was concentrating.'

'Not at all, that's fine.' The manager sounded hoarse and croaky. 'I did mention that you're excused from admin duties. You're free to just do Lohengrin, and then relax—do whatever you like.'

'I understand your concern. I won't do anything that could affect my performance as the Swan Knight, so there's no need to worry.'

'That's not what I'm getting at. What I mean is, I don't want you to be overloaded with menial tasks when you're already under a lot of pressure.'

'But this is my true calling,' Karl explained. 'This is where I feel I can relax. To be honest, it's not easy to sing Lohengrin knowing that all those people in front of their TVs are tearing me to pieces.'

'That's understandable...' With a harried frown, the manager shoved a hand through his hair, which was now more silvery-white than grey, and looked away. Deep furrows formed between his brows. The manager was about the same age as Karl's father, but he looked much older. He fished out a pair of gold-rimmed spectacles from inside his jacket and flicked through the pile of scores that Karl had put down a moment ago.

Karl saw that the manager was intently scanning for the authoritative notes in red ink. The great Wagner did not sign his name. But after his red ink touched the page, no one dared add anything further. He had the power to silence all composers, with a music that was beyond question.

'Well, don't push yourself too hard,' the manager said.

'I won't. And also,' Karl threw in casually, 'there's the forthcoming new work, which I'd like to be involved with as closely as possible on the creative side.'

The manager flinched ever so slightly at the words 'new work'. He was a veteran producer, so of course he hid it well, but he did have feelings.

Karl could tell he was rattled and vulnerable. 'I understand there have been a few holdups.' He retrieved his antique swallow-tailed coat from the floor where it had fallen when he stood up, and added, in a tone of idle chitchat, 'On the maestro's side.'

There was only one man known by that title at the Festspielhaus: Wagner.

The manager nodded with equal nonchalance. 'Yes, indeed. Still, the mind of a genius works in mysterious ways. We don't have anything specific to go on yet ... it's hard to say how things will pan out. I'd love to know what's going on in the maestro's mind.'

'There can't be much doubt about that, surely?' Karl bluffed outrageously, as if he knew all the details. 'What sort of directions are you getting?'

The manager inclined his head but again he avoided saying anything definite. 'Since it's you, take a look at this.' He riffled through to a particular page and pointed to the writing in red ink. 'This seems to give some indication? Of what's going to happen ... where we're headed.'

They shared a look of complicity. Slowly and deliberately, Karl slipped on his well-worn tailcoat, which had seen better days, and settled it onto his shoulders.

'We'll discuss this again, Karl,' the manager said in a low voice. He retraced his steps, taking the scores with him. There were people in the machine room—he must have sensed their presence and thought it best not to be overheard.

Sure enough, Gottfried and Hans entered as the manager was leaving, and waited for his footsteps to recede.

Once the door had thunked firmly shut behind him, Hans whispered, 'The bait's been taken.' He flashed a large brown envelope. 'The pirate station got an enquiry.'

'Well, we get a few calls a day for "Ludwig the singer", but this one seems legitimate,' Gottfried said moodily. That was his usual manner when discussing anything serious. He could only lighten up when talking about things that didn't matter.

'They're only asking how to get in touch with the singer to offer him a gig, though,' Hans qualified. 'But it's from an opera house above ground. And not just any old opera house. The Bavarian Court Opera House!'

'The problem is whether it's really from the Bavarian Court,' Gottfried grumbled.

Hans said, 'My contacts can look into it, but that may take time. If it's genuine, great! Time to catch the big one.'

'And if it's not genuine?' Gottfried demanded.

Hans shrugged. 'Sling our hook.'

'Can't we wait for another bite?' Gottfried asked. 'Or do you have something else in mind?'

'Wait a minute,' Karl cut in. He wavered for an instant but felt he should go on. 'I have something I'd like to put on the table. Of course, I want you to treat this as confidential, as all our dealings have been up to this point, or with even greater confidentiality.'

Gottfried said nothing, but there was a hint of arrogant discontent on his face.

'Of course,' Hans replied quietly, and motioned for Karl to continue. His blond-grey locks hung forward raggedly over his cheeks, half hiding his eyes. But Karl was convinced that

Hans would never betray him, no matter what. After all, it was exactly the kind of interesting story Hans would get a kick out of.

Karl plunged in. 'Sorry I didn't mention this earlier. I didn't bother because I didn't think it was worth bringing up in the first place.' He paused. 'Now I'm starting to think it may be a lot more serious than I first thought. There's someone, here in the underground, that I want to find. A man who may be even more pivotal than the Court Opera House or Prince Luitpold. I should warn you, there's a chance we might discover something we'd be happier not knowing.'

And with that, Karl began to describe the strange man who had strayed into his studio.

Chapter Twelve

'The Festspielhaus? Oh, okay then, go this way...' said Gottfried, taking care to sound casual.

Gottfried had strolled along in a flamboyant retro jacket, with a sheaf of music and a conductor's baton under his arm to make it obvious he was from the theatre. He was dressed like a portrait of Mozart, in a red brocade frock coat with lace peeking from the cuffs. He hadn't wanted to wear such an old-fashioned, ridiculous outfit—what era is this from?!—but he'd been overruled. According to Hans, frock coats were still worn by the chamberlains at court. And he had argued that 'what's-his-name' would respond to a retro look.

Then, just as Karl had said they would, a woman with a man who fit the description provided approached Gottfried to ask if he knew the way to the Festspielhaus.

Gottfried gave the pair only a cursory glance. 'Turn left, and when you get to the junction, take the way that is discreetly marked; then if you go down the twelfth side-tunnel on the right, you'll see several stairways, and the longest one will take you down to the lowest level. That's where the stage door used by the orchestra is: it's the third door along.'

After Gottfried had seen the odd pair on their way, he

joined Hans and Karl to add the finishing touches to their trap.

Chapter Thirteen

He couldn't be certain what he was doing that day. Was he dreaming of an underground labyrinth as he took part in the royal council, or was he dreaming of the royal council while he wandered through dark passages and narrow machine rooms? He couldn't remember. The soles of his feet hurt.

The one thing he could be sure of was that he wanted to meet Wagner.

And he could be sure of his friend, who wanted to meet Wagner too: Parsifal. Sword in hand, shielding him from harm as she strode through the world of darkness, she was beautiful and true.

A fine velvet ribbon, which she must have picked up somewhere or other, was braided into her hair. Colours were not well defined under the dim subterranean lighting. The ribbon was probably a dark shade of red or purple that verged on black. The vague contour of the matte velvet ribbon intricately interwove with the lustrous sheen of her cascades of black hair; it lent elegance to the still childishly simple lines of her cheeks.

As Parsifal held her lantern high, scanning the terrain ahead with the daring of a swashbuckler, a rift opened up between her fierce valour and her budding feminine allure. But the overall effect was not incongruous or absurd, but unexpectedly bewitching. Hers was a true beauty—there was no calculation about it whatsoever. She was well-nigh flawless.

For a wild instant, he would feel tenderness for her. He longed to take her hand ... no, he wanted to embrace her. But as soon as that image arose, it would be tainted by disgust. The feel of a woman's bare skin, the scent of her innermost body, and the unknown emotions lurking in those depths, jumbled together with unfortunate previous experiences, filled him with dread.

But her easy smile whenever she looked back at him, and the way she moved, like a carefree young warrior who only existed as an ideal, would captivate him all over again; he found himself trapped in a perpetual cycle of attraction and aversion.

They came to a halt in a labyrinthine room that branched out into seven or eight passageways, and Parsifal pointed to a tiny chalk X on a narrow archway. 'I think it must be this way,' she said. 'It's marked. So, what that good-looking conductor told us holds up. But why did he trust us with the directions so easily: did he think we were theatre people? Maybe we look like professional musicians. I hope that's it!' She held her lantern up to gauge what lay ahead. 'Let's go.'

Ludwig had no objection. The thought of meeting Wagner made his heart beat so fast his head spun. Euphoria made him groggy. He had to rely on Parsifal to get him there. He could no longer recall the directions. They went down some stairs, turned a corner at some point, passed through a room, went down the stairs...

All at once a panorama opened up before him. No, they

were still in the middle of a low-ceilinged corridor, which was as dimly lit as ever. But it was immediately obvious why he felt his field of vision dramatically expand. Down at the end of the straight, square corridor, which was perfectly empty—in stark contrast to the usual clutter underground—a TV had switched on.

Ludwig and Parsifal halted in their tracks—they hadn't noticed the TV until then. With the rasping roar of a sandstorm, its curved square screen brightened, casting a soft sheen onto the walls; black and white particles began to coalesce into a human form.

As they stared, the ambiguous form resolved into Lohengrin, the Swan Knight, in full armour.

'*Welcome to the Festspielhaus,*' Lohengrin said, in the mellow voice that Ludwig knew so well. His voice always sounded far too gentle—thin, at times—to be a heldentenor.

Deep in Ludwig's chest, his heart, which was already under a great deal of strain, sped up. Sweat beaded on his skin.

The Swan Knight... The Swan Knight is talking to me.

Lohengrin had his helmet tucked under his arm, and his other hand rested on the hilt of the sword at his waist. His armour flashed like silver scales at his smallest movement.

'*That way.*' Lohengrin took his hand off the sword to point to their left. The end of the corridor, where the TV sat, was a T-junction, not a dead end. Lohengrin was telling them to go left. It was like a fantastic dream! His mind lifted with dizzy exaltation, a feeling like being gloriously drunk.

The Swan Knight himself would lead him to Wagner! He felt intense fear and self-consciousness, but these feelings merely gave a keener edge to his joy, and the prospect of a still greater joy. At once he went to step into the corridor on the left.

'Ludwig, wait!' Parsifal gripped him by the arm. 'Something's off. Don't you think it's kind of weird? I mean ... Lohengrin, on TV, talking to us... It's bizarre. It could be a trap!'

'A trap—what?' Ludwig scoffed, in spite of himself. It was ridiculous. What was she so worried about? How odd that she mistrusted Lohengrin, one of the knights of the Holy Grail most renowned for virtue! 'You're not thinking straight, Parsifal. If you too are one of the knights of the Grail, how can you doubt the word of your fellow knight? If you dare not go, I'll go on alone. I trust the Swan Knight, and I trust Wagner, his creator, even if this is a trap. I would gladly fall into any trap set by Wagner.'

Parsifal's lips curved sadly. She was so beautiful. Her sorrowful smile shifted into the brave resolve of a knight of the Grail, and despite her delicate beauty, she held a threat like a slim blade. 'Okay. I'll come with you. I gave you my word, didn't I? That I would protect you.'

They walked on in silence, side by side.

Let's go, Parsifal, Knight of the Grail, and Lohengrin, the Swan Knight. To Wagner. To the one who reigns supreme.

Ludwig had never felt like this before; he was buoyed up by a rush of happiness and anticipation. The constant, nagging pain of unrequited longing was gone. Maybe it was just him, but the narrow, claustrophobic corridor seemed to widen as he ventured further in.

Around the next corner the light brightened again, and he could hear the noise of another television. The Swan Knight beckoned. Ludwig heard music; he could detect the TV signal running through his body. The signal, like a divine revelation, issued directly from Wagner. He bathed in it, absorbed it, as if televisions responded within his body. Behind the screen were all his dreams, his idols. Black and white ecstasy.

The TV was on and Lohengrin beckoned.

Chapter Fourteen

'Just a little further... Don't look away! You have to make it look like you're watching them. Don't speak yet. A little further ... wait ... okay, next line of dialogue.'

Constantly glancing at the surveillance camera monitor that showed the corridor, Gottfried was directing Karl, who was standing in front of the camera.

Karl had completely thrown himself into the role of Lohengrin with a far more commanding and lordly presence than he had managed for the music-drama filming sessions. He was finally free of all his embarrassment and self-doubt.

Hans's plan was to lure them into a seldom-used storage room, a secure location where no one would walk in on them.

'That door is the entrance,' Karl pronounced. 'If you wish to enter, the key is—' He broke off mid-sentence as total darkness swallowed them.

All the power had been cut off.

Chapter Fifteen

The TV went blank; Lohengrin vanished.

Ludwig was startled but did not falter.

This was a shrine to Wagner. Nothing could go wrong here. All that was meant to be would be. Right on cue, the near dark that had fallen was relieved by a faint, faraway glow, as if to guide the two of them. As if to invite them in. It was a gentle, ruddy light. He walked on, not bothering to watch his step. There was no need. Everything would be fine. This was a sacred place.

The light strengthened as they approached. The corridor filled with ruby radiance as it led them in, ever deeper. Here and there, television sets sat on the floor or hung from the walls and ceiling; from their screens, angels and gods gazed down on Ludwig, glanced back at him over their shoulders, peered into his face.

He could hear music. A piece by Wagner he had never heard before. Music like a fragrant blend of jasmine and orange blossom: a Wagnerian susurrus.

After a while the clusters of televisions thinned out, and the passageway gradually broadened. The music expanded to fill the wide, open space, its echoes reverberating ever further and wider. The light in the vast hall brightened towards a rosy pink alpenglow, wavered for an instant, then sank into periwinkle hues. The vault of the heavens was pale blue, tinged with lilac. White columns, which stretched up from the multi-coloured marble floor into the clouds above, appeared to be made of soft cream. A breeze blew; delicate petals brushed past his cheeks.

Beyond the columns, a lone figure stood.

The music modulated to a higher key. Ludwig headed straight for the far-off man.

As he drew nearer, he could see that the man stood behind a mixing console, lined with countless indicators and slide switches, on the other side of a tiny, limpid pool, still as glass.

The man had silvery white-grey hair, and a pair of gold-rimmed spectacles sat on the bridge of his nose. '*Welcome to the Festspielhaus,*' he said, as Ludwig approached. The same line Lohengrin had delivered.

'*You may wonder who I am; however, my name is not important. I merely serve Wagner, as one of the many anonymous workers behind the scenes,*' the man said, leaning forward to place his hands on the edge of the console. His voice was hoarse and gravelly but surprisingly well projected. '*How may I help you?*'

Before Ludwig could answer, Parsifal pushed past and placed herself in front of him—as if to shield him from attack. 'I am Parsifal ... oh, no, I mean ... please call me Ellie. I was wondering if you might be able to use me as a singer...'

It was a terrible shock. No longer did the holy knight stand before him. The girl was just a no-name wannabe, playing up her boyish charms to get a foot in the door. A sell-out! Instinctively he seized her arm, as if to stop her from fading away. Parsifal—who was actually Ellie, the wannabe singer—angled back toward him, a guilty and fearful look showing amid the stray tendrils of hair that framed her face.

'*I see. You may put your name down to audition when the theatre posts the next open casting call. Is there anything else I can help you with?*' Wagner's nameless employee said, his manner indicating that the conversation was coming to an end.

'I am here to see Herr Wagner,' Ludwig stated bluntly. He would not falter at the final hurdle.

'*Wagner does not receive visitors.*'

'Is that so?' Ludwig snapped. 'I am the king of Bavaria—'

'Don't question him!' Ellie told the man, her clear soprano tones cutting through Ludwig's outburst. Golden light shimmered down from the sky. 'He is—'

'*I know.*' Wagner's employee nodded.

What the hell did this jumped-up lackey think he knew? 'I am King Ludwig of Bavaria!'

'*Yes, certainly, Your Majesty,*' the man replied matter-of-factly, betraying no surprise. '*However, I am afraid that Herr Wagner does not receive visitors. Would you be best pleased if he were the kind of man delighted to dance attendance on the rich and powerful?*'

'Well ... but, but I'm...'

'*You're special: is that what you mean to say?*'

Ludwig shunted Ellie behind him and stepped forward, his toes dipping in the water of the tiny pool, to confront the man behind the console. 'Exactly. And there's no point discussing it. Only Herr Wagner himself would understand.'

'*Yes, I understand precisely what you want to say. That's what everyone says—that their love for Wagner is very special. They all talk about how well they know his work, how much effort they put into musical and textual analysis, the details they recall, the subtleties they grasp. That Wagner would understand. They all say the same thing. Everyone and their dog, exactly the same thing. It's a well-worn script.'*

The man's words pummelled Ludwig like blows to the gut; bile rose in his throat. The water at his feet broke into choppy ripples. He planted his feet firmly on the ground, fighting off wooziness. 'No, you don't understand. In reality, if he met with me...'

'In reality, you say? Oh, so what is reality, anyway? Are you sure that reality is worth believing in...?'

'I'm not here to debate amateur metaphysics with you. There's no need for smoke and mirrors.'

'What smoke and mirrors? Isn't this a fundamental question? We can't begin without first defining reality. If your reality is not clearly defined, meeting Wagner "in reality" might not mean anything to you. Is reality so dependable in the first place?'

'Indeed it is. Just as my existence, here and now, is a solid reality.'

'Your existence—is that genuine reality, as such? What if this were not your only reality?'

'Nonsense!' Ludwig blustered. 'Ask *her*, if you like.'

'Her? To whom are you referring?'

Was the man taunting him, or was the man a lunatic? Ludwig turned back to Ellie—

—at least, he attempted to. There was no one there behind him. Just the soft light of dusk, flickering over the green garden where sweet fragrance and music flowed. No one to be seen, near or far.

'Parsifal ... Ellie!' Ludwig shouted, looking about frantically. 'Come back at once! This is no time for tomfoolery!' Whenever he moved his head, he felt dizzy. A blur of drowsiness descended on him, dulling the vertigo. 'Ellie!'

'*Who on earth are you looking for? Your Majesty. Did you expect someone to be there?*'

'Of course I did! Weren't you talking to her just now? You told her to put her name down when there was a casting call!'

'*I have no idea what you're talking about... But apparently, this is what reality is like for you. For example, if I do this...*' The man took his right hand off the console and snapped his fingers. '*...the world is transformed.*'

Ludwig found himself standing on top of the sea. Startled, he tested the surface with his foot; it trembled, but he did not sink. Shafts of yellow sunset light were refracted by the undulating waves, sparking a blinding profusion of colour. Pink, orange, purple, and blue ... a show put on by the sky. He could take flight from here. If he let himself believe he could. The waves shone as if strewn with polished sapphires. With some effort, he kept his feet on the surface of the water.

The man was still calmly watching him from behind the mixing console. '*This is,*'—he snapped his fingers again—'*your reality?*'

Poisonous purple irises and cadaverous white lilies, trapped in a greenhouse. Their stems grew and tangled around him. He was slowly suffocating in their dreadful stench.

'*Reality, is it?*'

With the crackle of a TV being switched on, the flowers vanished, leaving behind only a whisper of scent, and he was standing in a garden on a summer evening.

'*You believe in this?*'

The moon loomed heavy over the ancient trees that now surrounded him.

Ludwig placed his hand on his heart to calm its hammering and struggled to master his ragged breath. The dizziness did not abate, but through sheer determination—and his royal pride—he held the man's gaze. 'What are you playing at?' he demanded. 'What tricks... You are mistaken if you think I'll be fooled by these illusions.'

'*Illusions—that's quite a claim!*' the man said coldly.

'Obviously they're illusions. There's no way they could be real!'

Until now the man had maintained an icy calm; for the first time, he let the corners of his lips turn up in a subtle smirk. '*So then, what is real? If you are ready to face it, you should take a closer look. What is your reality, Your Majesty? What does "reality" mean for you, fundamentally speaking?*'

The fellow was talking as if *he*, Ludwig Otto Friedrich Wilhelm of the House of Wittelsbach, had lost touch with reality.

Suppressing his agitation, Ludwig dragged in a breath and let it out again, deliberately slowly. His body felt very heavy. He lifted his eyes to the stillness of the night sky and felt the ground tremble beneath him. The vertigo refused to subside.

His breath hitched in shock. *What is* that?

A crack had opened up across the night sky—at least, that's what it looked like. Something in his mind shrieked: *don't look at it, you mustn't.* But what *was* it? The red-black fissure branched out, ever widening—no, it had been there all along. Another voice whispered: *come on, you know, you always knew what was going on.* Where was he? What was he looking at?

Determined to face his forebodings, Ludwig fixed his eyes on the crack. Better to plunge straight in than wait for catastrophe! But against his will, his eyelids lowered to obscure his vision. He was in a bad way. Acid bile crept up, rose into his oesophagus. *Cold, so cold.* Through the crack in his eyelids, he caught a glimpse of TV screens.

Sometimes it was better not to know.

This a fainting fit coming on? he was hazily wondering, when someone gripped him by the upper arms, as if to brace him up, with firm, warm, enveloping strength.

'*Open your eyes!*' It was a fierce mutter, low into his ear, in a thick Saxon German accent. '*In nowise credit that man's words.*'

In fear and trembling his eyes flicked wide open. Standing before him was a small man, no taller than his shoulder. Piercing grey eyes. Luxuriant sideburns leading down to a neck beard. A large beaky nose and a slightly protruding chin...

Wilhelm Richard Wagner.

The sacred likeness was living, breathing, present—right there before him. Ludwig had dreamed of and fantasised about this moment countless times, and every time he had thrilled and trembled like a virgin, but when the crucial moment finally arrived, all was calm. He was filled with quiet happiness. There was nothing to fear. It was merely a moment in time that was inevitable.

'*Don't dwell on what my employee said,*' Wagner repeated, with kind reassurance in his voice. '*I hope you can forgive him. He was only doing his duty.*'

'I know. I know...' The right words wouldn't come. His mind was serene, but tears flowed freely down his cheeks.

'*Come along, let's go,*' Wagner said. '*I've been awaiting your arrival. We profit nothing by staying here.*' He renewed his firm, warm grip, on Ludwig's right hand.

Chapter Sixteen

The theatre manager looked down from behind the mixing console at the large man lying on the floor. Rolls of flab bulged his filthy worker's overalls out at the seams; he had a wild tangle of ringlets and a thick beard that obscured his heavy jowls. It was definitely the exact same man who had wandered into the studio Karl was at work in.

Karl moved a little closer to examine him. The man's lips were moving feebly, and under his sagging lids, barely visible slivers of bloodshot eye white twitched. He was not unconscious; he seemed to be in a dream state. He looked happy.

The screens in the central control room were all displaying images of an unremarkable landscape. A black and white landscape. What was unusual was their sheer number. Dozens of monitors—actually there had to be over a hundred—covered the walls on both sides from floor to ceiling, and more were suspended from the ceiling. Their brightness was all that saved the huge room, which had not a single light on, from being plunged into darkness.

The theatre manager exhaled briefly and flicked a few switches on the console. Most of the screens went dark. Karl felt a hot tide of embarrassment rise up his neck: he was horribly out-of-place in his shiny stage armour.

'Thank you for not interfering.' The manager looked first at Karl, and then at Hans and Gottfried. 'Although I'm afraid I interfered with your plan. Sorry I cut the power with no warning.'

Who was going to respond? Hans gave Karl a sharp look—an unambiguous command to speak on their behalf.

'Not at all,' Karl managed. 'We are the ones who should apologise. We just ... heard there was a strange character going round searching for the Festspielhaus, so we thought we'd mess with him... It was a stupid game. Sorry.'

'That's quite all right,' the manager replied. 'It's enough that after I cut the power, you kept quiet, came here, and watched without saying anything. This guy requires careful handling. You must've wondered what was going on.'

'Yes, well,' Karl said. 'I think I get the gist. The ... he took what he saw on TV to be reality? Although that's hard to believe. How's it possible? How could anyone be taken in by trickery that's so completely obvious?'

'It's just that the three of you are new, so you don't know yet.' The manager sounded like he was exerting himself to answer a sensitive line of questioning. 'This man, you see, is unbelievably susceptible to TV screens. It's not the first time he's come here.' He shrugged. 'He's been coming two or three times a year, for the last few years. And every time he does, we let the clinic know to come and pick him up.'

So saying, the manager pulled a telephone out from the corner of the console. While he waited for the operator to put him through, he went on apologetically. 'But this is the first time he's brought someone with him. And such a young girl, too. It was like she instinctively knew how to handle the poor guy. Seems she played along with his fantasy of being a king.'

The manager must have clocked their uneasy looks. 'Oh, don't worry about her,' he reassured them. 'She's in another room. Someone from the office will be getting her story. Apparently, it came as a shock that the so-called king didn't even notice her being escorted out right before his eyes. Well, I guess the real shock was that he was in much worse shape than she realised. In any case, it wouldn't be good for her to carry on as she was with him, either...'

The call was put through, and in a routine manner the manager began to relate what had happened to the party on the other end. He might be speaking to a doctor. Perhaps a nurse, or a family member.

Karl knelt down beside the big man and took in his face, which was shining with unfathomable rapture. Hans came around the console to stand next to him. Karl turned to look up at the older man, who had a sad slant to his mouth.

'It'll be okay,' the manager told them. 'They said they'll be here to collect him soon.' Putting the phone down, he looked down at the man on the ground, seemingly at a loss. The studio scenes on the monitors—all from Wagner's music-dramas—lit up the stark outline of an obese man of middle years in the darkness.

Perhaps moved by pity, Gottfried plucked a cape-like garment from among the costumes, which were invariably strewn around any TV studio, to cover the man's fallen form.

The manager kept talking. 'So, anyway, we don't know what kind of illness it is. The nurses don't seem to be privy to the whole story either. It's a nuisance when he shows up here, but I feel bad for him ... because I don't think he knows—that the king known as Ludwig the Second of Bavaria doesn't exist.'

Karl swallowed back a fleeting impulse to dispute this.

'What are you talking about?' Gottfried gasped.

The manager gave them a rueful look over his spectacles. 'That's exactly it: most people wouldn't notice. But if anyone took the time to think about it, they'd soon realise. It might not even be a secret, actually. As it's so obvious. If anyone took a good, hard look at any recent footage of the "king", or even before that, if they paid any attention to what's been broadcast over the years rather than letting it wash over them, it should be glaringly obvious. The "King Ludwig" on TV is a mishmash of re-edited footage from when he was young. The real king, if there still was one, would be well into middle age by now. He ascended to the throne some ten or twenty years ago, maybe even earlier—it was a long time ago. Right?'

Gottfried started, struck by a sudden thought. 'But then there could be a real middle-aged king who governs behind the scenes. And the "King Ludwig" we're shown on TV must be government propaganda.'

Karl lost his patience. 'I think you're half right, half wrong.' He turned to Hans for the go-ahead, and Hans gave a subtle nod. Presumably—no, definitely—Hans knew the whole story. He had known everything, and he'd been using Karl, Gottfried, and the Festspielhaus for his own ends.

'Sir, I believe it was you who didn't notice,' Karl said sombrely. 'This man *is* the real King Ludwig.'

'What the...? Nonsense!' the manager scoffed.

'It's not nonsense.' Hans took over. 'He who lies here is the real King Ludwig the Second of Bavaria. I did wonder if I'd see him underground, but I never dreamed I'd have to confirm his identity.

'So, you must be wondering who I might be then, theatre

manager. Karl and Gottfried will be aware by now that I'm not merely a dilettante bit-part player. I'll come clean with you, as these are facts that all Bavarian subjects will come to know eventually, or at least should know. Actually, I want you to know.'

Hans continued. 'Let's just say I'm on the Prussian side. The Reichstag has had a number of problems running the empire. We needed to gauge the true condition of a king who never travels abroad or grants direct audiences, and whose only link to the outside world has been the limited footage released by the Bavarian government. More than twenty years have passed since he came to the throne. There are other monarchs and cardinals who only like to appear for public consumption in footage from their younger days, but King Ludwig was the only one not seen in the flesh for such a long period of time. Was he even still alive? For many years, we made overtures to the Bavarian government to be granted a royal audience, but they stymied us.

'Berlin considered various ways to reach the king, and I chose this one. I knew that even if King Ludwig abandoned politics, changed his taste in castles, and got bored of his young men, he would *never* let go of Wagner. As I expected, I got a few leads here. We already knew about the search for a "new king", which everyone here believed was for a forthcoming music-drama. Prince Luitpold has been looking for a royal body double for TV. All I did was use the rumour to my advantage. And you guys must've gotten a kick out of it as well?'

The flabbergasted manager must have called to mind the video clips Karl and the others had put together: he brought one up on the console and played it for them on a small monitor. 'I'm still a bit lost, but I think I'm starting to understand. These clips that've been run by pirate stations lately, Hans ... if that's the name you want to go by ... you had Karl and his crew make them? I figured it was Karl singing.'

'That's right,' Hans confirmed. 'That's what I called the "bait". I thought that when we put this out there, Prince Luitpold would show his hand. I didn't expect Karl to catch an even bigger fish.' He looked down at the big man sprawled out on the floor.

No one had expected to catch a real king. Or that the king would be so unwell.

Hans—or the man known as Hans, who was probably an imperial aristocrat with a grandiose title and an Iron Cross—stooped down to the prostrate king, who still had the look of joy on his face, to ease his breathing by slightly adjusting the angle of his head. 'To bring the king of Bavaria back to reality and involve him in the running of the empire ... would be impossible, given the state he's in. Now that I know that, my mission is complete...

'It looks like the only way to force Bavaria's hand is to let this be known widely, all throughout Europe, and to denounce Prince Luitpold, who must be holding the real power. I've sent my men to investigate all those who inquired about our bait. It's only a matter of time before they reach the secret film studio the prince has been preparing. They may have already located it. If this all comes to light, it could turn into a costly international dispute for Bavaria. If only the king could stay in his right mind at a time like this...' As Hans shook his head, the black-and-white light from the television screens gleamed among the waves of his hair.

Wagner music-dramas poured from the televisions, a mix of music that murmured over Karl, Hans, Gottfried, and the bewildered manager. Cables stretched between the monitors; equipment piled into mountains as though each piece controlled the others. Dark screens that led to other worlds.

Karl had a sudden flicker of insight into King Ludwig's mind. On television, there were dreams that could be safely surrendered to. Something that was a fiction through and through would never betray you, unlike reality.

Collecting himself, the manager said matter-of-factly, 'So, Hans, your mission is complete. Will you return to the world above ground, or back to your homeland, Prussia? If so, you can stop by the office and pick up your final wages. Though I'd guess it's a pittance.'

'I'll do that. Wish I could stay on as a dilettante chorus knight...' Hans didn't sound flippant; he meant it.

A short silence fell, which was broken by the phone ringing to announce the arrival of the medics. The team of nurses reached the depths of the Festspielhaus in a twinkling on the large props lift and left the same way. The scene of the king, carried out by eight bearers, was reminiscent of Siegfried's funeral. The king might have been pleased by that, if he had known.

Once the king had been carried out of the control room, Hans said somewhat wearily, 'Guess the nurses aren't in the know either.' An unnaturally intense chemical reek lingered in their wake. They must have given their patient a sniff of some dubious substance to ensure he wouldn't wake up in transit. 'What about Wagner—does he know about the king?'

The theatre manager didn't realise straight away that the question was directed at him. Defenceless dismay flashed over his face as he started and turned to Hans. 'About that ... I can neither confirm nor deny. A single word from me could spark off endless rumours. I can't take the chance that his new work might be further delayed as a result.'

Karl risked opening his mouth. 'Surely that's unlikely.' If he didn't speak up now, he might not get another chance. 'On the contrary, the new work should progress faster than ever now. I have a vision for a new part for the girl who was with the king, if she's any good as a singer. It'll all work out, I promise.'

'Karl, how can you be so sure?' the manager asked.

'How?' Karl paused. 'You must know how.'

'Perhaps.' The manager cleared his throat. 'Okay, I see what you mean. No doubt the new work is not too far from being officially announced. Karl, in many ways, this could mean a lot more work for you...'

'I don't mind. Honestly, I can't wait to get my teeth into it. If I could be excused from *Lohengrin*, I would have more capacity to assist Herr Wagner.'

'We should be able to arrange that.'

A brief but clear sign of understanding shot between Karl and the manager. Karl picked up his helmet from where he'd left it on the floor and turned to Hans with new confidence. 'Let's get going, while the office is still open.'

The three of them parted ways with the manager, and in silence they navigated the convoluted route from the control room to the office, to pick up Hans's wages, and then took a lift that would bring them to the upper levels. Once inside the box, which rose at a ridiculously sluggish pace—where no one could overhear them—Gottfried cornered Karl as if he had been waiting impatiently to do so. 'Karl, when you were talking to the manager just now, what was that all about? What were you talking about?'

'No big deal. Backroom shoptalk.'

'If you're going to play innocent, I'll come out and say it. I've had suspicions for a while now. Fill me in. You must've picked up on something? And the manager all but admitted it. That's it, isn't it? Come to think of it, there's an obvious explanation for all of this.'

Gottfried went on eagerly. 'I've always wondered ... if the manager might actually be Wagner himself? He acts like a dogsbody among dogsbodies, and claims to be at Wagner's beck and call when he gives his orders to the singers and the orchestra, but isn't the guy actually Wagner? You saw right through him. And he admitted it too. Am I right?'

Karl gulped and held Gottfried's gaze steadily. He couldn't deny that Gottfried had gained a degree of insight into the truth. Not many others would have guessed so far.

He could let Gottfried believe that, although it might weigh on his conscience. He could keep the truth to himself, so that he alone could savour it. That's what he'd originally intended to do. But the landscape had shifted since then. Soon, perhaps within the year, the king who lived in a fantasy world would abdicate and usher in an era of more practical governance. Change would come to Munich's underground city as well.

Karl shook his head. 'No, Gottfried. He's not Wagner.'

Gottfried, who had the self-congratulatory air of someone about to uncover a mystery, and Hans, who merely looked on without betraying any particular interest, were both caught off guard by Karl's calm confidence.

'He's not—then who is?' Gottfried demanded. 'Do you know?'

'Of course. I know it for a fact; it's not a guess or a rumour. I'm sure he's not Wagner. Because there is no such person as Wagner.'

No one said anything. The only sound was the dull hum of the lift, as it creaked laboriously upward. Gottfried half opened his mouth, which was missing his usual cocky pout, but closed it again.

'The manager and I found out the truth, only very recently,' Karl explained. 'There might've been a composer by the name of Wagner once. In the beginning, I mean. But now, there's no one who goes by that name.'

'No way...' Gottfried trailed off, lost for words.

'I'll tell you how I found out,' Karl went on. 'I'd been submitting my ideas for scripts and scores to Wagner, just like you and everyone else here. I'd heard that all the scores were developed through a process of collaboration: everyone checked and developed everyone else's ideas, and somewhere along the line Wagner edited to create the final draft, which was then passed on to the copyists; when I first joined this workflow, I believed that was exactly how it worked. But because I was arranging the full scores and copying out the parts that were passed on to me, I soon twigged—no matter what anyone else did, the ideas I added were never altered by anyone. Whenever I spotted a draft that needed work, I corrected it in red; the next thing I knew, my notes had come to be respected as Wagner's personal seal of approval, or disapproval, and no one dared touch them. This made it seem like "Wagner" was accepting my work unconditionally.

'Something was definitely off. I knew my work was better than anyone else's, if I do say so myself. But Wagner didn't take me to task for my presumption, nor did he praise me. The longer this went on, the more it bothered me; I felt I had to get a reaction from him somehow, and so one day I tried writing "Final Version!" on a score. It was treated and performed as the definitive version wherever it went. I thought I'd be found out for sure when I wrote "This man and no other!" on my *Tannhäuser* demo tape, but on the contrary, I was given the part of Lohengrin, which put me in a real fix.

'The others would come up with ideas, and I'd write, this is good, this bit is no good, here you need to do this —no one ever overrode me. Ultimately, before I knew it, I had gained full control over the output of the Festspielhaus. I knew my work was good, so once the trend got underway, I didn't hang back. By the time I started singing Lohengrin, I was convinced that Wagner's music was crowdsourced from a group of people who didn't know that they were the only ones creating all the different versions and arrangements. And now I effectively have total say over the Festspielhaus.'

Out of nowhere, Karl lost it and burst out laughing. Gottfried gave him an odd look, but he couldn't stop for quite some time. 'Sorry,' he finally managed, gasping for breath. 'It's just so crazy to think about. The most ridiculous part is, I just now realised that it must've been me who set off the rumours about the "new work". It's too much! I'd been hearing the rumours every day for months on end, and I still didn't click! You know the music in the control room, the instrumental piece that was playing when King Ludwig fell under the spell of the TVs—that's mine. I'd completely forgotten about it. I wrote that piece before we got jobs at the Festspielhaus—I didn't have any particular purpose in mind for it.

'I had it tucked away in my drafts folder for ages, but I lost track of it, and I was too busy to hunt it down. It must've gotten mixed in with a draft I submitted when I was really new here. A few people must've seen it—I guess the manager had the orchestra rehearse it, and that was the recording that was played in the control room. I remember I made a lot of notes on that draft; about turning it into an opera, what the story might be, et cetera, all jumbled together. And some thoughts on a totally new, original part. I don't know how many people saw it, but as everything gets passed around to everyone under the Festspielhaus system, it definitely travelled beyond the manager and me.

'I remembered it when I heard it playing in the control room. I hadn't realised that the score wasn't in my possession anymore. It didn't circulate back to me—I guess one of the directors hung on to it—so I never found out. I don't know if it's ridiculous, or pathetic... Actually, I should be happy. I guess I'm happy but I'm still getting my head around it. I was fooled by rumours set off by music I'd written myself, I got mixed up with a Bavarian government conspiracy and the plot of a Prussian spy, and ... I finally uncovered the truth about King Ludwig and Wagner.

'I think the manager put two and two together when we spoke just now. If that girl who wanted to audition is any good, Wagner's new music-drama will be written and completed in the not-too-distant future. I have a vision for it now. It'll be based on the legend of the Holy Grail and tell the story of the knight-errant Parsifal the Innocent. The overture will be the piece we heard in the control room, naturally!

'The manager asked how I could be so sure the new work was on the way. Of course I'm sure; I'm the one writing it!'

The lift juddered and came to an excruciatingly slow stop. To get to the surface, they would have to go down the passageway through the factories and take another lift. Karl pulled open the accordion-folding lift door to let Hans and Gottfried through.

The racket of the factories, which had begun to register a while back, would be deafening when they passed through a few more doors. To his musician's ear, it was usually an overwhelming din, but now it sounded like unfamiliar music with infinite potential—the art of noise. There was music in every sound in the world. Elation filled him, as well as self-doubt and fear in equal measure, but the fear would spur him on to create fresh melodies and arrangements.

'That's far enough.' Hans forestalled them from going all the way above ground to see him off. 'Especially you, Karl—you're not dressed for it.'

He was right. Taken aback, Karl glanced down at the shiny Swan Knight armour he still had on, and Hans grinned.

Hans pressed the slim purse of his earnings on them and practically forced them to take it, insisting that it should go towards production expenses for the music video. 'So, are you two going to be "Wagner" now?'

'No way!' Gottfried replied, laughing. 'I've set my sights on a more respectable career path. Karl's the one who's going to be Wagner.'

'I'll be in the studio for the time being,' Karl said quietly. 'I'd rather not sing. Am I going to be Wagner ... I don't know. I'm going to write a new music-drama, at least. If the work is attributed to Wagner, that's fine by me; if it's under my name, that's fine too. But I don't want to go public as the new Wagner. I'd prefer to avoid any future visits from eccentric royalty.'

Nevertheless, Karl felt for the poor man. Could there be anyone else who loved music as much as the king did, who longed so passionately, who devoted themselves so wholeheartedly? And had there ever been music as deeply loved as this, that could become a kind of religious faith, or a *raison d'etre*? Music summoned from the mystic abyss, beyond anyone's control; music that bore the name of Wagner. In the end, music was just a series of high and low pitches, a sequence of the same old intervals. But he was awed by the mystery of how this could affect people, take over their lives, and consume their minds.

Karl registered that he had been standing there in a daze, caught up in vague aspirations and musical motifs that lacked direction. But now, all the music in his mind had fallen into place, like the mystical instant when a ray of inspiration shoots through unconnected melodies and harmonies to channel them into a single composition.

Where did the power lie, in a mixture of sound waves that were organised in time? Karl was conscious that he had a fraction of that power, that people sometimes called destiny, within his grasp. That's when he realised—that he might define the destiny of some other unknown person, as Wagner did for King Ludwig. That this could be a love that was a stronger bond than the usual sense of the word that people used lightly.

Karl pulled himself together. 'And I don't want to sing on TV and be pelted with eggs and beer bottles anymore.'

Hans didn't laugh. He gave a pensive smile and a tiny nod, as if he had picked up on Karl's thoughts. And then, with only a passing farewell as though they would all meet again the next day, he strode off with the gait of a genuine soldier.

Karl and Gottfried watched him go in silence, and without a word, they turned back toward the Festspielhaus down in the deeps. *Better get a move on*, Karl thought. He couldn't wait to get back and fling off the fake armour. And after that, there would be a tonne of sheet music to work on.

Chapter Seventeen

As soon as Ludwig was back in his private royal quarters in the palace, he let out a sigh and switched on the television.

There was a cheap and nasty crackle, and the screen brightened with a buzzing drone. He dimmed the gaslights, changed into a robe, and sank into his armchair.

Wait half a minute for the big glass tube jammed inside the cabinet to warm up, and other worlds spread out before you. All sorts of dreams and all his idols dwelt within the black and white screen.

Ludwig fixed his eyes on the TV, without a single glance out the window at the beautiful lake under a dusky sky. Ever clutching the device tethered to the television by a vinyl-sheathed wire—a 'remote control', it was called—he drifted from dream to dream. His soul plugged into the television, along with the remote control...

A Wagner music-drama. It was about to start. He switched on his tape recorder, which he had set up with great care. It was now hooked up to a recording cable gifted to him by the Prussian envoy, so he no longer had to worry about background noise when recording. He'd long forgotten what the diplomatic negotiations had been about (probably the same old empty courtesies, anyway), but for some reason the one vivid memory that stayed with him was the unusually solicitous expression of the special envoy, Duke Hans Bernstein. The duke had shown a degree of sensitivity and thoughtfulness which would not have been out of place for a visit to a dethroned, imprisoned king.

The music-drama was *Parsifal*.

Strong feelings swept over him; yearning and Sehnsucht mingled with deep satisfaction. The overture evoked a nostalgia so immediate, it was hard to believe it was the first time he had heard it. Euphoric, he wanted to savour every note like a beautiful memory.

This was true happiness. This was what it would be like, when what he had sought for so many years was finally within his grasp. The young woman who played the lead role of the holy knight gazed at him from behind the screen with eyes that were resolute and yet shone with vulnerable innocence.

He didn't know why, but he felt a surge of nostalgic affection for her. He couldn't remember ever feeling so much affection for a female creature. As long as she was in the world, he felt shielded from all manner of hostility and evil. He almost missed her. As though he had buried memories of talking with her and fighting by her side, memories that were struggling up to the light.

Parsifal played the role of a fool who knew nothing, but her innocence saved the world. In place of the ailing, abdicated king, she ascended to the throne as the Grail Queen, prayed to the Holy Grail, and unveiled the Holy Lance to the world.

Such a perfect world. Such music. It blanketed his reality and made him forget everything else. Everything was just great. Here was a dream that was perfection layered on perfection. A sublime heroic figure. Yes, on a TV screen…

Sunk deep in rapture, Ludwig was falling asleep before he knew it. The floor was cold under his feet, but it didn't bother him; his body had grown heavier, sicker, and more sluggish than ever. His fading consciousness was consumed by the sweet ache of a desperate yearning. A craving so strong that perhaps no one had ever wanted something this badly.

I want to meet Wagner. The sublime musician, a man not of this world.

Love could be a lie, a cruelty, an excruciating torture. But one day, his dream would come true. Of course it would.

He didn't know why, but for some reason he was absolutely convinced of that.

Acknowledgements

I would like to offer my sincere, heartfelt thanks to the following people.

To my brilliant translator and colleague, Sharni Wilson. To my outstanding and visionary publisher, Francesca T. Barbini. To Kashima, an illustrator with an exceptional aesthetic sense, who created the cover art for this book. To my colleagues and friends in the Luna Family. To all those involved in the production, distribution and sale of this book. To you, my readers and friends through the medium of books. And to my beloved late husband, Toru Inoue, who passed away suddenly in June of 2023.

Discover Luna Novella in our store:

https://www.lunapresspublishing.com/shop

Milton Keynes UK
Ingram Content Group UK Ltd.
UKHW012137080524
442411UK00022B/114